No Cause to Kill

Why did she die? No one who had known her could even suggest a reason. Middle-aged, plain, virtually the invisible woman, Pauline Rourke had been the last person in the world to inspire enmity in anyone, by all accounts. And yet someone had killed her – killed her swiftly and viciously, in a public place. Why?

Instead of the usual plethora of suspects, in this case there seems to be none at all, and Lieutenant Meredith of the New York Police Department faces the task ot solving an apparently motiveless crime. Patiently he follows a trail that leads from the rarefied heights inhabited by the very rich to the squalid depths of Hell's Kitchen. The investigation widens in scope, involving more and more people, exposing more and more secrets, but without uncovering the murderer of Pauline Rourke.

Then, just as the trail seems to come to an end, a sudden turn of events has the effect of dialling the combination of a safe, and the murderer is forced once more towards a deed of violence – for motives that are skilfully and dramatically revealed.

This is Diana Ramsay's third crime novel featuring Lieutenant Meredith. Like its predecessors, it scores on three points: sound plotting, excellent characterization, and of course the way she writes.

by the same author

DEADLY DISCRETION
A LITTLE MURDER MUSIC

No Cause to Kill

Diana Ramsay

The Crime Club
Collins, 14 St James's Place, London

William Collins Sons & Co Ltd
London · Glasgow · Sydney · Auckland
Toronto · Johannesburg

First published 1974

ISBN 0 00 231569 6

Set in Intertype Baskerville
Made and Printed in Great Britain by
William Collins Sons & Co Ltd Glasgow

PART ONE

A BLAZING SUN was scorching the sidewalks of Fifth Avenue, and pedestrians moved wearily, encumbered with jackets, sweaters, coats, and a general superfluity of clothing. An exception, walking lightly in cork-soled sandals and looking comparatively cool in a white silk blouse and beige tussore skirt, was a slim woman with a pallid face and short, crisp dark hair liberally threaded with grey. She was not the sort of woman who would have attracted attention in the ordinary way, but today she was drawing baleful stares. Each time she intercepted one, her rather prim mouth quivered with the start of a smile that got no further.

She stopped to wait for the traffic light to halt the stream of cars separating her from the monolithic Victorian edifice that was Longfields department store, and the man standing next to her, red-faced and perspiring in a flannel suit, gave her a sidelong glare. This time she had to bite her lip to suppress her amusement. If looks could kill – Well, he was uncomfortable. Everybody was uncomfortable. The calendar said April, but Apollo had evidently got his wires crossed.

The light changed. Darting across the street and up the steps to the store's portico, where there were golden interdictions of NO SMOKING painted on the glass doors and tall, sand-filled urns to make compliance convenient, she had to wait for three women to exit. The third let the door swing to in her face. A good case could be made out for revolving doors, even in so conservative an institution as Longfields, if somebody were interested in making out a case. Somebody else. As far as she was concerned, revolving doors were a treat for kids and a drag for everybody else.

It was cool inside and, predictably, very crowded. Inching forward, she reached Handbags and stopped before a fawn-coloured capeskin pouch with an olive-wood buckle on the flap. Italian, of course. And astronomically priced, of course. But one of those things lovely enough to make considerations of price an irrelevance. As soft as it looked? She stretched out a hand, drew it back. Not now. Perhaps on the way out, if there was time. It required thought.

She moved on, heading for the escalators. Not the quickest way to get up to Five most days, but today the wait for an elevator would be interminable. At least on the escalator one moved, however slowly. And one could always look down at one's feet, so as not to be deflected from one's purpose by the tempting displays of merchandise. Particularly now, nearing Three – Household Wares. Not so much as a glance at the pots and pans today. Purpose was the printed lawn awaiting her in Fabrics. If it was still there.

For the next lap of the ride, she transferred her eyes from her own feet to those on the step above. On the left, flaring denim trousers and construction boots – college girl. On the right, a pair of expensive, gleaming brown calf pumps with stacked leather heels, the legs above trim and just a hair's breadth too skinny. What was behind? She cast a discreet glance back over her shoulder, and only with difficulty restrained herself from turning round to stare. Saddle shoes. Brown and white (very dirty white) saddle shoes. Of all things! Who wore saddle shoes nowadays? Who, apart from kids, had ever worn them in the past? These, clearly, belonged to no kid. They were huge, distended by bunions; they supported painfully swollen legs encased in surgical stockings, like overstuffed sausages that would pop as soon as touched. Œdema, very likely. Poor creature.

For the last lap, it was safe to look up. Carpets. Not a department Longfields was noted for – or deserved to be. Leaving the escalator, she traversed an aisle between piles of rugs without a glance at them. Fabrics was next. She by-passed laces, silks, and velvets, and marched up to the counter where cottons were displayed. Ginghams. Voiles. Lawns. She cast her eyes over the bolts of lawn.

Where was her lawn? Not out on the counter where she had seen it last time. Nor could she spot it among the bolts ranged on the shelves behind the counter. The post here being temporarily deserted, she stepped behind for a closer look at the shelves.

'Can I help you, madam?' The query, uttered at her elbow, was disapproving, charged with disdain for customers who usurp prerogatives.

'You *may*.' The stress, though not great, struck her ear unpleasantly. The salesgirl was not in the wrong: she was. Mitigating her own display of disdain with a smile, she returned to the proper side of the counter. 'I'm looking for a print I saw here a few weeks ago. Blue flowers on a white ground.'

'This one?' The salesgirl instantly drew a bolt of lawn from the top shelf and laid it on the counter.

'No. The flowers were much smaller. And the blue was darker.'

'I know the one you mean. I believe we sold the last of it. But I'll check.'

'Thank you.' Left to herself, she bent over the counter to take a closer look at the lawn she had spurned. No, it wouldn't do. Not even in a pinch. Such big flowers of so bright a blue would overpower the subtle dark blue *pesante* of the suit. Too bad she hadn't had the foresight to pick up the other last time. But she had not figured on needing a blouse; had planned on the suit's seeing service at the theatre, at concerts, at places where there was no need to remove the jacket. No way of anticipating the coming week-end, and the necessity to present herself as both elegant and *en famille*. A blouse would solve the problem. Definitely. If it was no go here, she would try Altman's and Lord & Taylor tomorrow.

Something other than lawn, perhaps? She made a rapid survey of the vicinity, her glance taking in fabrics and skimming almost sightlessly over people. But then her eyes were caught and held by a woman standing only a few feet away. A tall, heavy, flabby-looking woman with a dissolute, disgruntled face and rusty red hair that needed retouching at the very grey roots (or better still a close haircut and a fresh start), wearing a filthy beige raincoat open over a blue seersucker dress that looked pretty filthy, too. An extraordinary sight in Longfields; doubly so in a department like Fabrics, with its specialist population of hobbyists, handy housewives, and smug possessors of 'good little dressmakers'.

Their eyes met, and the rusty-haired woman averted hers with a suddenness nothing short of furtive, as though her mere presence on the spot were some sort of crime. Then she turned tail and waddled off on grotesquely swollen legs – the very same legs observed on the escalator. No mistaking those saddle shoes. What on earth was a woman like this doing in Fabrics? She looked as though she wouldn't know what a needle was for. But perhaps she had a handy sister. Or daughter. No, not a daughter – impossible to imagine her a mother. Unfair. The condition of those legs was enough to account for any amount of disgruntlement; any amount of self-neglect. Probably heart trouble was the cause. Or liver. Or kidneys. Or all three. Poor creature.

'Sorry to be so long, madam.' The salesgirl was back. 'We're all sold out on that particular pattern and so is the manufacturer, unfortunately. Will any other do?'

No other would, she informed the salesgirl, and expressed thanks. Nor would any other fabric in the whole of Longfields extensive department do, it seemed, though she was tempted by a blue silk *ombré* plaid accented with narrow stripes of mauve and emerald green. For a moment she visualized a blouse with a large, soft bow at the throat and then, with a faint sigh, dismissed the vision. Not her sort of thing. Not at all her sort of thing. Fifteen years ago, perhaps, but not now. Superannuated spinsters were better advised to stick to floral prints or – if they felt really daring – polka dots. Not that she was all that crazy about polka dots, but it was sobering to think that soon she would be past them, too. Well, if tomorrow's expedition to Lord & Taylor and Altman's failed to unearth a nice print, she could always resort to polka dots. Live it up.

She left Fabrics and again passed through Carpets without a glance at the wares. Nearing the Down escalator, she hesitated, then veered towards Bridals. Might as well take the opportunity to use the lavatory, as long as it was handy. It would be crowded, undoubtedly, but so would the office lavatory, invariably the scene of a stampede during lunch hour. Here, at least, she would be spared the confabulations of switchboard girls and receptionists.

Not so very crowded after all: they were standing only two or three deep outside the cubicles. She joined a line of two, and immediately the cubicle ahead was vacated and she was able to move up a place. What luck. Like breaking the bank at Monte Carlo.

Suddenly, she was jostled from behind. Something pricked her right arm. She jerked it away, and felt resistance in the silk of her sleeve. 'What on earth – '

Her arm was grasped firmly above the elbow, pricked again. Pricked? Jabbed, rather. She turned her head and then, as her arm was abruptly released, swayed. The black and white checkerboard floor seemed to come up to meet her. She caught a glimpse of dirty, misshapen saddle shoes and swollen legs, moving away. She tried to regain her balance.

Difficult. Very difficult. She felt dizzy. God, how dizzy she felt all at once. Her arm was burning, but the rest of her was cold. Now her head was pounding. And her heart seemed to be going a mile a minute. Thump, thump, thump, thump. Deafening. And her breathing – She couldn't catch her breath. All the while the checkerboard was moving. Or was the problem with her? A scream reached her ears as she toppled: it sounded thin and faint and distant, like the noise of a train that was pulling away.

'Imagine going like that. No warning. Nothing. One minute she's standing in the john as quiet as you please, minding her own business, and the next – boom! What a way to go! Just thinking about it is enough to give you the willies. That's the way it is with heart, though. It could happen to anybody. You. Me. *Anybody.*'

'You're not kidding. I went hot and cold all over when I heard.'

The conversation was carried on in hushed, portentous tones by the girls behind the Bridal Linens and Bridal Lingerie counters, both of whom looked young and fresh enough to model for advertisements of their wares. Their eyes were on the door marked 'Ladies' two aisles over, where a policeman in uniform stood on sentinel duty.

'You know what I think?' Bridal Lingerie began. 'I think – '

The approach of a customer silenced her. A male customer, young, looking slightly dazed and more than slightly embarrassed.

'Can I help you, sir?' Bridal Linens got in first.

'Yeah, you can.' The young man turned his back on Bridal Lingerie with a sigh of relief. 'My buddy's getting hitched and I have to buy a gift. They told me all I'd have to do is walk in here and somebody would tell me what to get. His girl's name is Armstrong. Ellen Armstrong.'

'Oh, *her*. I'm afraid we can't help you here, sir. You'll have to see the Wedding Bells shopper.'

'What for? All I want is – '

'Miss Armstrong has her full quota of soft goods. You wouldn't want her to have a surplus, would you?'

'Why not?' The young man was showing fight. 'She can always use another tablecloth, can't she? Look, miss, I'm on my lunch hour. Couldn't you just – '

'I'm sorry, sir, but we can't help you here. You'll have to see the Wedding Bells shopper. Down the centre aisle and to your left.' A majestic forefinger pointed; a haughty stare outfaced a glower and a spate of inaudible muttering. Then, as the young man dashed away, the forefinger came down on the counter with a click. 'The nerve of some people.'

Bridal Lingerie did not comment. Her attention was riveted on the door marked 'Ladies', which was starting to open. She sucked in her breath with a soft, choked gasp. 'Here they come!'

Through the door came two men in white hospital coats carrying a stretcher, the form upon it swathed in blankets, followed by a uniformed policeman and a young doctor, who was scowling and fingering the stethoscope around his neck as though it were a string of worry beads. The procession, augmented by the sentinel, moved swiftly towards the service elevators and was soon lost to view. A collective sigh reverberated through Bridals: the vigil was over.

A private, echoing sigh from Bridal Lingerie. 'I thought they'd never come out of there.'

'They were pretty quick, when you consider all they must have had to do,' Bridal Linens said. 'What do you bet every female customer in the store suddenly feels the urge to pee?'

'Oh, Ruthie, you're awful. Did you happen to take a good look at that doll of a doctor? He was real worried about something. You know what I think? I think he's so young he still gets upset at the sight of death.'

'You and your romantic ideas. He's probably wondering what his girl-friend is up to when he's out answering emergency calls.'

'Oh, Ruthie, you really *are* awful.'

The young doctor's brow failed to clear during the descent to the street; during the march to the ambulance, his play with the stethoscope became almost frenetic.

Now and again he cast a sidelong glance at the policeman beside him, as though hoping to be asked something, anything, but the policeman, a phlegmatic, middle-aged man with a wad of tobacco stuffing one cheek, asked nothing. The doctor watched stretcher and stretcher-bearers climb into the ambulance, put one foot inside, then took it out and turned to face the policeman.

'Look, I hate being a buttinski, and it's not that I'm trying to climb on to anybody's raft, but – ' He hesitated.

The policeman shifted his wad to the other cheek. 'Spit it out, son.'

'Well, I think this could be something for you. From what the eye-witnesses say, it looks like a pretty straightforward heart attack. You couldn't call her a girl and I've seen it take them a lot younger than that. One thing's a little funny, though. She wasn't mainlining, but there's a mark on her arm that could be a puncture mark. Also a scratch and a pulled thread in her sleeve. Could be she ran into a stray hatpin somewhere and it has nothing to do with anything, but – ' A shrug. 'Maybe my imagination is working overtime, but I'm thinking it could have been an injection of something to induce cardiac arrest. I know they're thorough at the Medical Examiner's Office and they wouldn't be likely to miss anything, but I can't see that sounding the alert can do any harm. Anyhow, pass it on. For what it's worth.'

'Dead? What do you mean, dead? She can't be dead.' The voice snapped over the wire – authoritative, brooking no contradiction, and sounding a note of grievance, as though the announcement of death constituted a personal affront. 'She went out of here as lively as a chick a little while ago. Left a whole batch of important letters to be typed and – ' A short silence, evidently for reflection, for when the voice spoke again it was milder. 'You say Miss Rourke is dead? You're sure there isn't some mistake?'

'There isn't any mistake, Mr Lefebvre.' Polite. Patient. Professional. But the speaker, a young man seated at a desk in a huge room sectioned off by partitions, was making a face at the opposite number who couldn't see him, as a child might. 'According to the documents in her handbag, she was Pauline Rourke, an employee of your – '

'Naturally she was an employee of my firm. She was my personal secretary. That's why you were put on to me.' Another silence. 'How did it happen? Some sort of accident, I presume. She told me she was going shopping during her lunch hour.'

'She did go. Longfields. That's where it happened. Not an accident. We haven't had the medical report yet, but indications point to sudden heart failure.'

'Heart failure? That's preposterous! There was nothing the matter with her heart. Why, she had a check up only a couple of months ago. The doctor pronounced her fit as a fiddle.'

The young man made another face. 'I'm not in a position to comment on that,' he said smoothly. 'She wasn't a young woman. Sometimes – '

'Forty-four. Approximately a quarter of a century younger than I am.' Asperity that verged on the bellicose. 'Well, I'm sorry to hear it. Thank you for letting me know so promptly. Now if you'll excuse me, I must see about getting someone to type those letters from Miss Rourke's notebook. They're very important.' The receiver went into its cradle with force.

The young man hung up, tipped back his chair, and

poked his head round the partition on his right. 'Hey, Abe, I just had a big shot corporation lawyer who's all shook up because his secretary kicked the bucket and didn't get her letters off. Inconvenienced him no end. Some people really have it rough, don't they?'

Abe clucked sympathetically.

' – no evidence of acute heart disease. All the indications are that death resulted from an injection of Dexamyl. One of the better known amphetamines. Overdose causes the heart to speed up so fast it gives out. Which isn't exactly news to you, I know. Not much chance it was self-administered because the puncture mark is too far back on the upper right arm. Some of the drug spilled on her blouse and on the skin around the puncture mark, so we probably won't have to run the full battery of chemical tests on the organs and you won't have to wait for the results while the trail gets cold. Isn't that lucky?' The voice that sent this information over the wire was fraught with gloom, which, apparently, not even luck had the power to dispel.

Red-haired Lieutenant Meredith of Homicide was similarly unaffected by the mention of luck: his gaunt, bony face wore its habitual expression of wary melancholy, with the shadow of a scowl at the ready. 'Sounds pretty fancy,' he said.

'It's fancy all right. Murder in the market place. Somebody who couldn't get access to her while she slept by flying in through her window like a vampire bat.'

'Or somebody who wanted us to think that.'

'You're the detective. Somebody who did a lot of planning, at any rate. Maybe the reason for choosing a public place was a hope that the thing would go as a heart attack and nobody the wiser. Somebody who believes all the stories about municipal inefficiency and doesn't know a standard procedure is followed in every case of sudden death under suspicious circumstances that comes our way. And if a puncture mark doesn't constitute suspicious circumstances – Anyway, no chance of missing this because somebody got clumsy with the needle, so clumsy that the hospital internist called in by the store spotted it right away and passed on the word. Definitely your baby.'

'Thanks.' The single syllable had overtones that set the wire humming.

'You're welcome.' The formula rejoinder was ironic. 'In case you don't know it, Mike, which you probably do, Dexamyl is pretty well known in mind-blowing circles. In small doses it gives a nice high, so they say. It's had a bit of press attention. Not as much as the mainline stuff and the more popular barbiturates, but some. That means it's available. To anybody.'

Meredith did not comment. He bestowed a scowl on the blank wall in front of him.

At the other end of the wire, a message was received. 'Well, at least you know it has to be a woman.'

'Do I?' A decided rasp in Meredith's baritone. 'How about a transvestite? Or somebody who put on drag for the occasion? Or somebody who's so with it that you have to take a second look to tell which?'

A brief silence at the other end. Then, softly, 'I'll get the report to you right away.'

The report on the post-mortem examination of Pauline Rourke stated, in addition to the suspected cause of death, that the deceased had been a Caucasian female in her early or middle forties, height five feet four inches and weight one hundred and twelve pounds, with grey eyes and dark brown hair approximately thirty-five per cent grey; that she had had no deformities or scars; that she had suffered from no diseases of the vital organs; that she had not been addicted to drugs; that she had been in the early phase of the menopause; that she had not been a virgin; that she had never borne a child.

Meredith was reading the report when Sergeant Drake, who shared the office, came in from a long stint of giving evidence in court, or, as he put it, 'sitting on my butt for five hours till they got around to calling me to the stand for five minutes'.

'Then you should be ready for action,' Meredith said. 'A good thing. We've got ourselves a lulu.'

Drake's broad, swarthy face, imperturbable as a rule, clouded over. 'Not the one they're talking about downstairs? The duel to the death with bicycle chains between the model high school students?' With two hostages to fortune growing up in Queens, Drake tended to react strongly to cases involving youth.

'No. Rosen has that. Ours isn't kids. Ours is a master mind who gives lethal hypodermic shots of speed in public lavatories.'

Drake guffawed.

'What the hell's so funny?'

'Well, you have to admit it sounds pretty ridiculous. Like a plot for a horror film. I can see Bela Lugosi gnashing his teeth as he drives the needle home.'

'You've been spending too many late nights in front of the television set with the kids. Not Bela Lugosi, unless he wore a wig. Elsa Lanchester, maybe.' Meredith heaved a sigh. 'Probably the baroque ornaments are covering up nothing more than the usual profit or passion motive.

Maybe she poisoned a neighbour's cat and the neighbour bears grudges. Chances are it's something that will stick out a mile before we've been on the job five minutes, and then we can let the DA's office worry about the ornaments.'

But no motive was immediately forthcoming from Mrs John Strazzera, the mother of Pauline Rourke, who was summoned by officialdom for the formalities, nursed through an outburst of sobbing at the sight of the body, and eventually installed in the hard wooden chair (softened temporarily by a cushion borrowed from a bursitis sufferer in another office) on the other side of Meredith's desk. Mrs Strazzera was built like her daughter, with a delicate bone structure and no superfluity of flesh, yet managed to generate an impression of softness that the woman in the morgue could never have approached. She was pretty in a curiously old-fashioned way, with a heart-shaped face, a pale but youthful complexion lightly dusted with floury powder, a froth of feathery blue-white curls, and an expression of timid helplessness that testified to a talent for dithering and none for concealment. Her reaction on the telephone had been one of incredulity; even now, after the proof, there was incredulity in her large violet eyes.

'I don't know what to say to you.' Mrs Strazzera had small, slender, almost clawlike hands, and they plucked at each other in her lap. 'I kept thinking you'd made a mistake, it wasn't Pauline at all, perhaps she'd changed handbags with somebody else, until – You must think I'm a nincompoop.' The last was uttered with resignation, as though being thought a nincompoop were a routine feature of her life.

'Not at all, Mrs Strazzera,' Meredith said. 'We realize

it's been a great shock to you. The mind sets up barriers against shock.'

'That's exactly right. You've expressed it perfectly. Thank you.' The little shower of gratitude and a fleeting, wan smile suggested that efforts to understand her were few and far between. 'It's so difficult to accept. You keep on thinking of them as children no matter how old they are. Although there was nothing childlike about Pauline, God knows. In fact, it sometimes felt as if she was the mother and I – She was so much more capable than I am. In everything.' The hands interrupted their plucking for a flutter. 'It's so difficult. I keep thinking – Her heart, you said it was. But there was nothing wrong with her heart, as far as I know. And she certainly wasn't old enough to be having coronaries.'

'You can have them at any age,' Meredith said. 'But I didn't tell you your daughter died of a coronary thrombosis, Mrs Strazzera. I told you heart failure, which was telling you exactly nothing. This is going to be another shock, I'm afraid. Somebody injected her with a drug that caused her heart to fail. She was murdered.'

'Murdered? *Pauline*?' The violet eyes grew enormous. Then, slowly, but with decision, Mrs Strazzera shook her head. 'That's impossible. Absolutely impossible. Nobody in the whole wide world would want to murder Pauline. I'm her mother. I ought to know. There's been some sort of mistake.'

Meredith assured her there was no mistake, patiently gave her a synopsis of the circumstances of her daughter's death, read out sections of the medical report. All to no avail. For so soft and vague a woman, Mrs Strazzera hung surprisingly tough, refusing to budge from her position: nobody would have wanted to kill Pauline and that was that. Yet there was no sign of the usual reason for resistance to the idea of murder, fear that all the family cupboards would open to expose dirty linen within. Far from it.

'I've read enough detective stories to know that when people get murdered the first thing the police do is look for a motive. Well, you're perfectly welcome to look to your heart's content. I've nothing to hide. I'll be glad to answer all your questions or do anything else you want me to do to help you. But I can tell you right now you won't find anything. Pauline was so – so harmless. She never interfered with other people. She carried minding her own business to such lengths that – ' The hands were plucking rapidly now. 'Even at times when you wouldn't have minded a little interference – just to know somebody cared – she wouldn't. She wasn't the sort of person to step on anybody's toes or get in anybody's way or anything like that. She simply wasn't. And of course nobody had anything to gain from her death. She made a nice living, but it was only salary. I doubt if she had much in the way of savings. The thought of her being murdered in that horrible way – '

Mrs Strazzera broke off, her eyes suddenly very bright. 'Something just occurred to me, Lieutenant Meredith. Couldn't it be that she was murdered in place of somebody else? I mean, if the ladies' room was crowded, whoever did it might have jabbed the wrong person by mistake. That's a possibility, isn't it?'

Meredith admitted that it was. 'Not the likeliest possibility, though. In any event, not the first one we explore. You can understand why, Mrs Strazzera.'

'Oh, of course. Perfectly. You know your job, I'm sure. I wouldn't dream of telling you how to do it. It's just that there's nothing about Pauline – '

Again Mrs Strazzera broke off, this time because of a knock at the door, and then, as a man in a black leather motor-cycle jacket entered the office, she heaved the sigh of one who feels many burdens lifted from her shoulders. 'Oh, here's Johnnie. I'm sure he'll tell you exactly what I've told you.'

John Strazzera carried himself like a man proud of his body, and doubtless his tall, muscular frame had once been something to be proud of, but now he had begun to put on weight and it was all going to his belly, a not very attractive bulge below his jacket. His chief asset was a head of thick and glossy black hair a man twenty years younger might have envied. Plainly he was some years his wife's junior. How many was hard to say, for the onset of middle age, blurring and softening, operated to close the gap.

Appealed to, Strazzera confirmed his wife's assessment of his stepdaughter's character, giving it as his opinion that no one 'had it in for Pauline'. Yet he was nowhere near so convincing as his wife; he seemed, to an experienced observer of reactions to murder, a trifle uneasy. Why? Private knowledge that contradicted his wife's? Guilt about something else? Or simply the discomfort felt by even the most upright of citizens when called upon to make statements to the police?

Mrs Strazzera, bolstered by the presence of her husband, was rapidly throwing off the last remaining symptoms of shock. 'You'll be wasting your time trying to find a motive,' she said, almost aggressively. 'Oh, I'm not saying Pauline didn't have her faults. She was far from perfect. She wasn't a particularly warm person. When she was only a little girl, she shut herself away from me and that was the end of it. From her brother, too. I can see somebody being bothered by not being able to get through to her, but not bothered enough to kill. No, you'll never make out a case for Pauline as a murderee. Not in a million years.'

The word 'murderee' showed that the influence of the detective stories went deep. Well, it was a way to play it. 'There's another angle to consider, Mrs Strazzera,' Meredith said darkly. 'People don't get murdered only because they make enemies. Often it's for reasons you might call occupational. Conceivably your daughter got herself mixed up in something that – ' He stopped.

For Mrs Strazzera was laughing. Laughing so hard that tears welled up in her eyes. A delayed manifestation of shock?

'You're barking up the wrong tree with that one, copper,' Strazzera said, and this time his conviction could not be faulted. 'Not Pauline. Bucking for a medal from the girl scouts, she was.'

Precisely where had John Strazzera run off the rails and been spotted by Pauline Rourke?

The section of Greenwich Village bounded by 14th Street on the north and 8th Street on the south, Fifth Avenue on the east and Seventh Avenue on the west, while not considered as posh a residential area as Park Avenue or Sutton Place, is popular with those moneyed enough to regard any area of Manhattan as within their means, the primary attraction being the soupçon of Bohemia that is lacking in the staid, ultra-conservative upper East Side.

Pauline Rourke's apartment was in a six-storey yellow brick building on West 12th Street. Not a new building.

Possibly, Meredith surmised, a rent-controlled building. Nothing fancy about the lobby – beige walls, brown leather sofa and a pair of matching arm-chairs, three standing brass ashtrays – and the elevator was self-service, but the building was well maintained. The superintendent, J. Vermeer, whose name appeared under his title in the slot beside his buzzer, was a grey-haired Negro with an intelligent, self-reliant countenance. He listened to the announcement of Pauline Rourke's death without surprise, and said only, 'I'm sorry,' looking and sounding as though he meant it. He escorted Meredith and Drake up to the fourth floor, unlocked the door of 4D with a key instantly located on the large, crowded key ring that came out of his hip pocket, and waved them inside. 'I guess I can leave you to it,' he said.

'That would be appreciated,' Meredith said. 'But I'd like to ask you to stick around the building for a while. We'll want to talk to you when we're through here.'

'That doesn't surprise me any. There's something funny about her death, isn't there?'

'Yes.'

'Figured something was up when the patrolman came by earlier and asked me to keep an eye open for suspicious characters. It wouldn't happen to be anything like murder, would it?'

'It would.'

'I'm sorry. I'm really and truly sorry to hear that. She was a decent sort. Look here, if there's any way I can help, just call on me. Though I don't really see how I can, still – '

'We'll keep it in mind, Mr Vermeer,' Meredith said. 'I take it you wouldn't have any ideas offhand?'

A headshake. Very firm. Very emphatic. 'Not a one.

Unless you'd call an opinion that Miss Rourke was the last person on earth anybody'd want to kill an idea. A most upright person. Kept herself to herself. Didn't entertain much. Seemed content with her own company. Didn't ask much of anybody. Or expect much. That's about all I can tell you.'

The small foyer inside the door struck a keynote – luxury without ostentation. The carpet was of thick, soft moss green pile, and on one cream-coloured wall hung an antique oval mirror with an intricately carved, gilded frame, the motifs of the carving repeated in the supports of the shelf below the mirror and in the sconces on either side; these last, holding light bulbs with frosted glass shades instead of the candles they were designed for so many, many years ago, were the only sources of illumination. The foyer contained nothing else. What else did it need?

To the left was an arch, and Drake, first to glance through to the living-room beyond, emitted a soft, admiring whistle. 'Did herself proud, didn't she?'

It was beyond dispute. The first thing that registered with Meredith, as his gaze swept over a spacious room of breathtaking beauty, was that the deep gold velvet drapes over the bay window opposite were open, and he went to close them, his footsteps soundless on the moss green pile. A soft sighing accompanied the glide of velvet over the curtain rod. He made a circuit of the room to switch on lamps and returned to the arch.

Now, by the artificial, indirect lighting, the room looked positively regal, always assuming that taste went hand in hand with rank. The sofa in front of the window, a graceful two-seater handsomely carved of pale wood and upholstered in heavy matte silk the colour of old burgundy held up to the light, was the throne; the two round satinwood tables on either side, bearing lamps of rose-coloured marble with pongee shades, were resting places for sceptres; the half-dozen chairs upholstered in ivory brocade, dusty rose satin, and pale green velvet were perches for subjects of distinction.

But to categorize the place as a throne was too summary, too superficial. The *pièce de résistance* was a burr walnut pedestal desk whose spare, simple lines and harmonious proportions provided a feast for the eye. It stood between a pair of tall bookcases with glass doors (holding mainly scientific treatises and a good representation of current thought in many fields, with scarcely any fiction and not a single paperback), and on the wall above was the room's only picture, a Degas drawing of a dancer arching her back as though trying to get the kinks out. Worth a smile. Worth a bit of money, too, very likely. On the desk was a black leather pad and on that an electric Olympia typewriter; in the drawers was an assortment of documents, correspondence, and stationery supplies. There were other signs that the room had been created for living, not for purposes of state. An imposing sideboard housed, not the expected showpieces of plate, silver, and crystal, but a Hi-Fi unit and a bar with an impressive array of bottles, including almost a full case of Teacher's Highland Cream. Just inside the arch stood a marquetry chess table, with ivory and ebony chessmen set out for a game in progress.

'They're no slouches,' Drake remarked, examining the chess game. He looked up with a puzzled frown. 'This sure as hell isn't what I expected to find.'

'Same here,' Meredith said. 'Still, we shouldn't be in any hurry to jump to conclusions. She was a legal stenographer, don't forget. That's always good money, and she was secretary to the senior partner. All this could have been within her means. I'm inclined to doubt that it's a job lot unloaded on her by some decorator. Care shows. And patience. And – well – devotion. Could be it all cost a lot less than ignoramuses like us suppose.'

'Kind of knocks me for a loop anyway. I guess I'm readier to believe that salary covered it than to believe she belonged to the what-the-wife-doesn't-know-won't-hurt-her class of secretary, considering what she looked like. But of course playing footsie doesn't exhaust the possibilities.'

'No, it doesn't.' Meredith made a careful, lingering survey of the room and turned his back on it. 'The longer I look at it, the more alive it becomes. Let's go see if the larder's stocked with caviar and pheasant under glass.'

A short hallway with two doors on the left and two on the right led off the foyer. The nearer door on the right, the first attempted, led to the kitchen, a room basically neither attractive nor convenient – tunnel-shaped, no more than ten feet wide and almost twice as long from the door to the single window, which was a tiny affair, high up on the wall and offering a view of a dreary little yard crammed with garbage cans. These disadvantages conceded, the room had nothing to apologize for. Yellow ochre walls, white-washed ceiling, and terracotta tiled floor set a tone of warm, cheerful rusticity, anachronistic, perhaps, with the up-to-the-minute sink, stove, and refrigerator, but somehow the collision of past and present broke no bones, set no nerves jangling. The magical blending power of personality, doubtless. A narrow board table and benches called to mind picnics in public parks (except that the open-air facilities were never of top quality pine, as these were), and on the wall above, hanging from iron hooks, were numerous cooking vessels of dazzlingly bright copper and enamel in every conceivable size and shape. A board-and-brick bookcase below the window held standard culinary works – Escoffier, Larousse Gastronomique, Mrs Beaton – and books by the likes of James Beard, Elizabeth David, M. F. K. Fischer, and Julia Child.

There were pine cupboards above the sink and the refrigerator, containing, along with enough crockery to service an army, a bounteous supply of tinned and bottled and packaged foods. The refrigerator, too, was well stocked. Meredith drew out a large earthenware bowl covered with aluminium foil. He lifted an edge of the foil, saw thin squares of meat marinating in liquid under a canopy of crumbled bay leaves, raised the bowl to his nose, sniffed. 'Beer,' he said, in response to an inquiring look from Drake, and replaced the bowl in the refrigerator.

'Sounds like a good idea, marinating meat in beer,' Drake said. 'I'll have to tell Eleanor about it. Pauline Rourke wasn't one for opening cans, obviously. Seems to have taken a lot of trouble about food. They usually don't unless they have a man to cook for.'

'I'd be more inclined to think she had an exacting palate. From the looks of this apartment, I'd say not mortifying the senses was a guiding principle of life for her.'

The next room explored was a combination den and spare bedroom, small, streamlined, modern in mood, noteworthy only for the good taste displayed. The carpeting was a basket weave of some substance with the colour and appearance of hemp but soft underfoot – most effective against oiled walnut, the only wood present. The convertible sofa was a sturdy, comfortable-looking model upholstered in a warm russet and orange tweed, and the two leather arm-chairs, one tan and the other olive green, looked comfortable, too. A unit of cupboards, drawers, and shelves constructed along one wall aroused Drake's admiration. It accommodated a sewing machine, a television set, a second Hi-Fi set, a second bar (half a dozen bottles of Teacher's here), a multitude of personal effects, books (plenty of paperbacks but again very little fiction), and a large collection of records. The last were at floor level, and Meredith squatted to take inventory. Classical music, virtually none of it vocal, with a chronology bounded by Bach at one end and Bartok at the other. Clearly the collection of someone who knew what she liked and felt no obligation to put up a front by pretending to like anything she didn't. But wasn't that the story of the apartment in general?

Oddly, this room, the most straightforward and unassuming explored yet, yielded the first real mystery. In the closet were about a dozen lounging outfits, several pairs of oriental pyjamas and the rest floor-length shifts with Pucci labels. All were far too long to have been worn by Pauline Rourke. Whose were they?

The mystery was dwarfed to insignificance almost immediately. At the spectacle that lay beyond the next door, Drake let out a fervent 'Jesus!' and Meredith sucked in his breath.

Pauline Rourke's bedroom was like a Hollywood set for a film about the idle rich, circa 1930. A Technicolor film. Sumptuousness here was not, as in the living-room, in the abundance and beauty of the furniture, for bed, bedside table, and chaise-longue comprised the lot and there was nothing special about any of them. Sumptuousness here was in the riotous parade of colours and textures; a magenta velvet bedspread against a headboard of quilted emerald green satin; a cyclamen shantung shade stretched like an umbrella over a malachite bedside lamp; a high-voltage *art nouveau* print covering the chaise-longue; cornflower blue wild silk draping the walls from ceiling to floor; royal purple carpet of pile so deep the foot disappeared in it almost up to the ankle ('Like walking into a snowdrift,' Drake commented).

If the effect upon the eye was stunning, the effect on the mind was no less so, and two experienced policemen who had seen almost everything were momentarily struck dumb.

And then Drake blinked and shook his head, like a man trying to clear away cobwebs. 'I think this has set me going in the wrong direction,' he said. 'The instant reaction was that it's the obvious, and all the bloodhound's hackles started to rise at the prospect of lacing into that superintendent for telling us she didn't entertain. But on second thought – ' He shrugged. 'I can't see it for orgies, in spite of the way it looks.'

'Not a single mirror,' Meredith observed.

'That's right. Who ever heard of an orgy without mirrors? But it's more than that, it's a sort of feeling I get. The thing is, can't see men here, harem trappings or no harem trappings. Any guy walking in here would feel – ' Drake hesitated.

'Overpowered?'

'Overpowered. Outclassed. And just plain ploughed under.'

'I get that, too. I also get a sense that it's all very private. It wouldn't surprise me to find out nobody but

Pauline Rourke ever set foot in here.'

'Me either. Well, maybe we're both nuts.' Drake went over to the wall and tugged at the draperies. They parted, revealing an alignment of doors. He opened one. A closet. Within, tidily arranged on padded hangers, were suits and dresses of subdued colours and conservative tailoring – clothes for a respectable maiden lady who understands her type and has no aspirations to stand out in a crowd. Other doors opened on shelves and drawers of lingerie, scarves, hats, handbags, shoes. Here again, nothing spectacular, nothing the proverbial crowd could not absorb.

Drake closed doors gently. 'You know, I'm beginning to get a whiff of Jekyll and Hyde.' He sighed. 'Very faint, though. Not strong enough to smell like murder.'

Detective Bill Alessandro had become hipped on antiques while still a patrolman, and the turning on had been fast. As fast as a day-long investigation of a robbery at an antique shop. Even faster, to hear him tell it. 'I took one look at the stuff that was left in the shop and flipped. But instantly.' The 'stuff' had included an attractive shop assistant who had illuminated the newborn passion with knowledge. She had not lasted. The passion had, and gradually Alessandro had come to be recognized as the New York Police Department's authority on antiques. Not (as he was the first to admit) that anybody was pressing him to look to his laurels, but he looked to them all the same. Passion was passion.

He sat now in Pauline Rourke's living-room with his legs crossed and his hands cupped around a mug of cocoa, the graceful green velvet arm-chair a bizarre background for his all-black apache attire (Meredith's message had reached him at home, after his day's tour of duty was over). He took his time looking about him, and his face was expressionless. Then he grinned, with a rather diabolical glint in his eyes. 'The purists wouldn't go for it,' he said.

Meredith, who knew his man too well to be enticed into a manifestation of surprise, waited for elucidation. He, too, was informally dressed, but his was the shirt-sleeved, loosened tie, buckling-down-to-work variety of informality.

'The purists would consider this room a jumble,' Alessandro went on. 'By their lights, it's a sin to mix periods, and she has a Sheraton desk and a Louis XV chess table in the same room.' His thumb jerked downward. 'Speaking for myself, I'd credit her with excellent taste and a sure sense of line and colour. She not only knew what she liked, she knew when to stop. A lot of them don't.'

'How much do you figure all this set her back?'

'Depends. Nothing here is the kind of item collectors chase with their tongues hanging out, but everything's worth a little something. I'd guess she couldn't have assembled the stuff in this room for less than ten grand, give or take a little. If she went through decorators, it would be a lot more. But I'd say she didn't. I'd say she was probably knowledgeable enough to do her hunting herself.'

'I had a friend who works in an antique shop come around to have a look a little while ago. She thinks the pieces were probably acquired one by one, over a period of time, so the outlay wouldn't have been all in a lump.'

'I'd go along with that. You don't put together a room like this overnight. Who's your friend?'

'Cassandra Evans.'

'I met her once. At an antiques show. Talked to her for about five minutes, but it was long enough to see she knew her stuff. You can rely on what she says.'

'I know that. But two opinions are better than one.'

'True. Did she dig this room?'

'Yes. Very much.'

'Anybody with any sense would, jumble or no jumble. It's a very personal room. It's alive. I can see Pauline Rourke stalking each and every item, waiting and watching for just what she wanted and swooping down on it. Paying what she had to pay to get it. I don't see her as the kind to snap up something just because it was going cheap, which is why I pegged it at ten grand.' Alessandro finished his cocoa and, before setting the mug down on the table beside him, wiped the bottom with his handkerchief. 'Listen, Mike, about that bedroom – Nothing there for the collector. Just a pretty weird place. Made me feel I was in the fun house at an amusement park, kind of. Maybe because of all the doors. But what really got me – Hell, it's a bedroom and the bed is big enough for any amount of action, but what kind of action? If any dame ever received me in a room like that I'd turn and run. To be crude about it, I can't even imagine getting a hard on in there.'

Meredith tried to suppress a grin (in the department, Alessandro's reputation as a stud was second only to his reputation as an authority on antiques) and didn't quite succeed.

Alessandro tried to look innocent (self-advertisement was not the source of this secondary reputation) and didn't quite succeed.

When Alessandro was gone, Meredith went over to the desk, which was blanketed with papers (the Olympia had been relegated to the floor), and resumed the task he had begun earlier, that of sifting and scrutinizing the dead woman's papers. But tonight, it seemed, he was fated not to progress very far. Before he had put in more than a few minutes' work, he was interrupted again. A key turned in the lock. Swiftly, he got up, snapped off the light, and went over to stand against the wall just inside the arch, prepared to see without being seen.

The door opened and closed. The lights in the sconces on either side of the mirror came on, and the reflection of the visitor appeared between them. A woman, tall and gaunt and striking of aspect. Dark, shoulder-length hair drawn straight back from a pale, lofty forehead. Widely spaced dark eyes set deep below arched eyebrows like strokes of a charcoal pencil. An aquiline nose with flaring nostrils. Full lips with the lower shaping a disdainful curve (habitual? or did the sight of herself bring it there?). A narrow but forthright chin. A handsome face, despite the lack of feminine softness. An unforgettable face. Meredith had definitely seen it before. What memory failed to dredge up was where.

Meredith stepped through the arch and into the foyer. Catching sight of movement in the mirror, the woman whirled on him with eyes that looked haunted – haunted by more than the sudden apparition of a stranger. For a moment, she contemplated him in silence, as though a stare from those eyes, reinforced by the deepened curve of that lower lip, had the power to make men quail, if not disintegrate on the spot. Perhaps it had, backed as it was by the authority of money. Lots of money. There had to be a substantial bankroll behind that magnificently tailored black leather trouser suit with the single zippered pocket below the belt of the jacket; behind the insouciance that walked the streets of New York without a handbag.

The silence lengthened, and, as it became apparent that Meredith was not going to break it, curiosity stirred in the woman's cavernous dark eyes. 'Who the hell are you?' Her voice was deep, its cultivated enunciation overlaid with a hoarseness that grated slightly on the ear. 'Don't tell me. Let me guess. A burglar.'

Without waiting for a reaction, she turned on her heel and strode into the hall. 'Save it,' she threw back over her shoulder. 'I have to use the toilet in the worst way.'

In a moment she was back, and again in a hurry. She strode past Meredith and into the living-room, making a beeline for the sideboard. She opened a door and took out a bottle of Teacher's and two glasses. 'What's yours?'

'Nothing at the moment, thanks.'

'Nonsense. Name your poison or like what you get.'

'Bourbon then.' Meredith re-entered the living-room, switched on a lamp, and sat down. She poured with a generous hand, filling the glasses nearly to the brim. A serious drinker, clearly. Where had he seen her before? Annoying not to remember. Galling to professional pride.

She came over to him, carrying the glasses with a steadiness that threatened no danger to the carpet, and handed him one, then retreated to a chair some distance away. Her eyes flitted over the desk, made a pointed examination of his shirt-sleeves, came to rest on his face. 'What kind of a burglar are you? You should have taken advantage of the opportunity to make a getaway. Under the circumstances I could hardly have obstructed you.'

'I'm not a burglar.'

'You astonish me.' An effortless swallow disposed of about a third of the contents of her glass. 'You look like official business of some kind. Very official. What is it? Snooping around behind Pauline's back to see whether she paid her income tax?'

'Even the Bureau of Internal Revenue couldn't get away with that one.'

'I wouldn't know. I've never had any contact with them. Somebody takes care of it for me.' She took another swallow from her glass. 'I can see fencing with you is a good way of getting nowhere fast. All right. I'm Ivy Eastbrook. That rings a few bells, I imagine.'

It did. It set bells positively clanging. The Eastbrook millions. Culled from the nationwide chain of supermarkets founded by John Eastbrook, dead this quarter of a century and more, who made his pile in the days before the Government took all, and left it to his motherless only child, Ivy Eastbrook. Or Ivy Eastbrook Cheyney, as the Press sometimes called her, though who Cheyney was or had been Meredith could not for the life of him recall. Neither could anybody else, very likely. No mere appendage had a chance for any part of the spotlight that had shone on Ivy Eastbrook almost from birth. Her exploits had made headlines. Her numerous exploits. Love affairs, feuds, out-and-out brawls, voyages across the Atlantic in sailboats, flights to remote regions of the globe in single-engine planes – you name it, she'd done it. Not recently, though. Recently she had become something of a recluse, tucked away on an island in the Bahamas. Or so the legend had it. Possibly the legend needed revising. For one thing, it made no mention of –

'We went to school together,' Ivy Eastbrook said, reading his thought. 'Amsterdam College. Which explains nothing, of course.' She finished her drink, got up, and went to replenish it, again filling the glass almost to the brim, again carrying it to her chair without spilling a drop. 'Fortification. Not that I need an excuse, but I have a feeling this is going to be rough. Where's Pauline? Something's happened to her, hasn't it?'

'Yes.'

'It's bad, isn't it? I can tell from your face. Is she dead?'

'Yes.'

The recoil, the spasm of agony that contorted the handsome features were genuine, unless Ivy Eastbrook was a consummate actress. 'Tell me,' she said.

Meredith did. In detail. The shock that flashed in her eyes at the mention of murder looked genuine, too. But of course the routine questions had to be asked, and the answers they elicited relegated them to the part of the routine that is filed away and forgotten. As a suspect, Ivy Eastbrook seemed to be out of the running, having been in her Bahama retreat for part of the day and in her airplane for the rest. As a source of possible reasons why Pauline Rourke had been killed?

'I'm utterly at a loss. Who would want to murder Pauline? The last person one would ever imagine – ' A quick gulp from her glass. 'You're sure you haven't made a mistake and – But you don't do things like that, do you? Put the wrong name to a corpse? Anything like that?'

'There are slip-ups occasionally. But not this time. She's been identified.'

'Her family, I assume. It must have been a dreadful shock for them. Such an inhuman way to die. Either it's the most malicious scheme of destruction I've ever heard of, or else some lunatic's running amuck and Pauline just happened to be the one to get caught in his toils. It could have been something like that, couldn't it?'

'You're not the first to suggest the possibility. But the bloodhound's instinct argues against it, or at least against accepting it right off the bat. The way we start is by sniffing around Pauline Rourke's life, and the spades and shovels come out when we get a whiff of anything unusual.'

'A subtle way of pointing the finger. But then I can see how I'd strike you as an odd sort of acquaintance for Pauline.'

'Acquaintance hardly seems the right word. You have a key. And the clothes in the closet of the guest room are yours, aren't they?'

'Yes, they're mine. I see that detectives earn their pay.' She swallowed more of her drink: stiff as it was, she had almost reached the end of it. 'I can guess what's going through your mind. What would be going through most minds. Forget it. Pauline wasn't a lesbian, and as for me, I've been accused of just about everything else, but not that. We were friends, that's all. I don't get along with many people, but I got along with Pauline. We latched on to one another in college and more or less stuck. That is, I stuck. There was nothing of the leech about Pauline, take it from me. I'm an authority on the breed.' Only the faintest trace of bitterness in the last.

Meredith did not comment. He did not prompt. He waited.

'You want more than that, naturally.' Ivy Eastbrook finished her drink, rose, and made the journey to the sideboard again, this time bringing the bottle back with her. 'It's difficult to explain why we clicked, mainly because I've never been clear on it myself. You couldn't call it a communion of interests. Pauline was a zoology major – science all the way. I was Fine Arts. What else would you expect of someone who could buy the contents of practically any museum in the world?' For a moment, a twist of the lower lip made the handsome face downright ugly. 'I suppose I might spare you the exhibition of self-loathing. I'll try to stick to the facts. Actually, saying we went to school together isn't strictly accurate. I didn't meet her till my junior year, when I transferred to Amsterdam from Sarah Lawrence. Pauline was a senior. She had the cubicle next to mine in the library. The partitions separating the cubicles were only waist high – the sight of somebody else's diligence was supposed to spur us on or something. The sight of Pauline's diligence was almost too much for me. A real beaver. Work, work, work. But even I could see that grinding away like that wasn't the usual effort to impress professors or make the Dean's List, though it accomplished both. It was truly a matter of subjecting herself to a discipline to get where she wanted to get. Admirable, of course, but I was far from admiring it. How could I? The perpetual butterfly who can't and won't settle to anything doesn't enjoy being forced to look in the mirror. I used to sit in the library wishing I had a stink bomb to set off under her nose. Until we became friends. Extraordinary that we ever did, really.'

'How did that happen? The inspirational power of a noble example softening a hard heart?'

'Don't be ridiculous.' Ivy Eastbrook smiled – a rich, warm smile that held nothing back. 'I started things going. It was a kind of game for me, seeing if I could lure her away from her books. I didn't succeed, and I found myself cheering her on for the way she parried the nuisance tactics. Always patient. Sometimes amused.

Never sore. People don't usually react to me that way, and I thought she must be playing a part and sooner or later I'd get under her skin. But I never did. It was years before I could admit to myself that she felt sorry for me. Imagine anybody feeling sorry for Ivy Eastbrook.' A shadow fell over the smile. 'The quality I valued most in Pauline was her absolute indifference to what made other people fall all over themselves to pay court to me. It wasn't a pose – she was totally without façade. She was the most self-sufficient, self-contained, self-controlled person I've ever known. I might as well throw in self-absorbed and selfish, even at the risk of giving you a wrong impression of her. But I don't suppose you're simple enough to mistake my meaning.' She emptied her glass and set it down beside the bottle. Her haunted dark eyes sent Meredith a challenge: Mistake my meaning. Prove yourself a simpleton.

Meredith passed it up. 'There's a mystery here that's been sending us round in circles. Maybe you can clear it up. That bedroom of hers. It doesn't seem to fit in with – '

'Isn't it a horror? Something for a Mafia Mother, if such an animal existed, but I guess there are limits to what the Women's Lib movement can accomplish. My nerves wouldn't survive a night in that room. But Pauline enjoyed it. She really and truly enjoyed it, poor thing. It was a kind of magic carpet for her, I think. An Arabian Nights of the mind. Strictly of the mind, contrary to what you're thinking. Not that Pauline didn't have her little adventures. Ancient history, though, and I couldn't tell you anything about them anyway. Pauline was no confider, and I was always too busy talking to listen. I can assure you the room wasn't a setting for orgies. But I suppose you're hardly likely to believe that on my say-so.'

'Hardly. But so far I haven't heard anything from anybody to inspire disbelief. You're being very helpful, Miss Eastbrook. There's one more thing that puzzles me. You said a minute ago that Pauline Rourke worked like a beaver to get where she wanted to get, and I assume you meant the scientific discipline. But she doesn't seem to have made use of it after college. Why not? It couldn't have been because of any lack of opportunities.'

'Astute of you to have picked that up.' She offered this grudgingly: astuteness from him was a clear disappointment to her. Pouring herself another drink, she flashed him a glance full of hostility. 'Drink up and stop looking so damned virtuous. I could tell you it's shock that makes me go at it this way, but that wouldn't be true. I generally go at it this way. The nice thing about Pauline was that she took my little quirk in stride. Didn't go all prissy. Didn't hurl those darts of disapproval, the way you're doing now.'

'I'm not hurling anything.'

'The hell you're not. Do you carry a gun, Lieutenant? Or a scout knife?'

'I carry a gun, Miss Eastbrook. The knife's at home in a bureau drawer. So is the manual.'

She smiled. Without enthusiasm. 'I guess I'd better lay off before you recite the pledge. You win. I'll stop being childish and get on with it. You said you thought it odd that Pauline should have packed in science after coming so far. Well, it was odd. It was perfectly extraordinary. She simply sat down one day to take stock of herself and came to the conclusion that her intelligence was second-rate. So she turned down offers of fellowships – good offers – because she thought the academic world had more than its quota of second-raters.'

'Sounds as though she was pretty hard on herself. How justified was the assessment?'

'She had a solid, retentive mind. Everything that went into it stayed there. But the ability to make original connections – No, she didn't have that. So you might say it was justified. What she did have would have been enough for most people to be going on with, but Pauline preferred to cut her losses and give her life a shape it could hold. I could never quite decide whether it was cowardice about tackling something too big for her or the display of integrity it seemed to be. One possibility doesn't exclude the other, I suppose.' Ivy Eastbrook took up her glass, drank from it, set it down empty. 'Does that sound fuddled to you? It sounds fuddled to me. You'll have to excuse me. I've had a dry day because I was flying, so the blur settles in quickly.'

'You're making sense. As much sense as anyone else I've talked to so far. What made the two of you stick together through thick and thin? The way it sounds, you've inhabited different planets since college. Or is that putting it too strongly?'

'No, that's putting it just about right. But saying we stuck together through thick and thin isn't. A few years after college I went off Pauline. Permanently, I thought. At any rate we didn't see each other for years and years.'

'Why?'

A slight hesitation. 'She knew me too well. Inside out. I suppose when you're young and dedicated to frivolity you like to think there's some mystery about yourself. There was never any mystery about me for Pauline. And then – ' Ivy Eastbrook's eyes made a circuit of the room, fell on the chess table, and darkened with pain. 'Do you mind if we leave it at that for now? It doesn't seem the right time. Or the right place.'

Meredith did not press it. 'How did you get back together again?'

'Drift. Wind currents. Phases of the moon. Who knows? We ran into each other somewhere one day, and we were both ready to take up the threads again. Perhaps I was more ready than she was, but then I was the one who always needed more. And after you pass a certain stage on the downhill slope it helps to have someone you don't have to put up a front for. Sanctuary, too. I've withdrawn from circulation, as you doubtless know, but I still rate attention, like a slumbering volcano, and in Bedford Hills or Beekman Place I feel the eyes of the world upon me. So when the wanderlust brings me to New York, I often hole up here.' The dark eyes were still on the chess table.

Meredith's imagination conjured up a vision: two women who had no need to talk to each other because there was nothing left to say seated at that table, concentrating on the game with an intensity that obliterated everything else. And, perhaps in response to the very same vision, perhaps in response to another, Ivy Eastbrook covered her face with her hands and began to weep with raucous, rattling gasps.

Contrary to popular belief, there is seldom any mystery involved in murder investigations. They are, in the general way of events, largely a matter of routine. Ask the standard questions, run the standard checks on the answers, and sooner or later – more often than not sooner – the police come smack up against the one person who was in the right place at the right time and bore the necessary complement of animus against the victim. Routine.

The girl at the PBX board at Oxman, Lefebvre & Styles was young and, notwithstanding bleached, much-teased hair and eyes shadowed with the green of the sea and outlined with the green of the forest primeval, looked reasonably stable (conceivably, a graduate of one of the parochial high schools from which large firms habitually recruit junior staff). She flicked switches with deftness and efficiency, spoke to the machine in careful, measured, ladylike tones. It was in far different tones that she cut off Meredith's opening words.

'Pauline Rourke? Oh, you can't see *her*. She's dead. Sorry.'

Again Meredith attempted to explain the nature of his errand; again he was cut off.

'Her office? You want to see her office? What for? It's just an office.'

Now Drake took over. Without verbosity, he managed to convey that thorough exploration of milieu was a routine feature of police investigations when there was a question of foul play. The green-rimmed eyes grew wide with wonder as the girl heard him out, but it was the stress on 'routine' that carried the day. Routine, it was clear, was a thing she understood; her resistance was to anything not part of her own.

Meredith and Drake were passed on to others. Several others. Further explanations were necessitated (though a full statement of purpose had been given earlier by telephone), including one to the head of the Oxman, Lefebvre & Styles typing pool, who had had, she confessed before she was asked, only minimal contact with Pauline Rourke. This explanation proved the most effectual, for the head of the typing pool handed them over to Miss Marjorie Jonas, a brisk, sensible-looking woman in horn rims and low heels, with neatly waved hair of rich chestnut brown that appeared natural but probably wasn't, in view of her age. Miss Jonas, who was secretary to Richard P. Styles, led the two policemen through a room full of gawking typists to the office that had belonged to Pauline Rourke, offering them all the assistance they required, yet, by her manner, making it abundantly plain that they were taking her away from more important duties.

'I can tell you straightaway that you're not going to find anybody around here who was on terms of intimacy with Pauline Rourke, so don't be surprised if asking questions turns out to be a waste of time. She wasn't gregarious, to put it mildly. She came in, did her work – did it extremely well, I might add – and went home again.'

'You make her sound like a robot,' Meredith remarked.

A slight unbending. Very slight. 'Well, no, I wouldn't go so far as to say that. It wasn't quite as bad as that. She attended all the office gatherings – didn't try to wriggle out of them the way some people do. And she'd sometimes come out to lunch with a group of the girls, though she preferred to bring her lunch and eat it in her office. She said she didn't care for luncheonette food, but a lack of sociability was definitely a factor. I knew her about as well as anybody here, so if you have any questions you may ask them of me.'

The offer was not immediately taken up, full attention being given to the surroundings. Pauline Rourke's office was, as advertised, 'just an office' – small and drab, the walls beige and the carpet brown, furnished with desk, typing table, file cabinet, and a couple of dark green chairs, all of modern design and looking new. There was not a single picture, knick-knack, or ornament in sight, and the only items that did not strike the note of mere utility were the window curtains of vivid burnt orange Siamese silk.

'She made them herself,' Miss Jonas said, observing and interpreting Meredith's glance. 'The ones they put in here after the redecoration were brown and yellow plaid, the same as I have in my office. She said she couldn't live with them and they let her change them. They wouldn't let her change anything else, though. She wanted a different kind of desk – offered to buy it herself – but they wouldn't go for that. Probably because it would have meant finding a place for this one. A lot of trouble for nothing. It's a perfectly good desk. All that on top belonged to her.'

'All that', neatly set out on the clean green desk blotter like a picnic feast on a carefully tended lawn, consisted of tortoise-shell comb and natural bristle hairbrush, Vademecum toothpaste and Vademecum mouthwash and natural bristle toothbrush, transparent plastic soap dish containing a sliver of white soap, a tube of Almay Complete Make-Up in a shade called Soft Ivory and an Elizabeth Arden lipstick in a delicate pink shade called Fragile, and a small bottle of Bufferin.

Meredith attempted to open a drawer of the desk, and failed. He tried another, and failed again.

'Everything else belongs to the firm.' A reprimand.

'The way you look after the firm's interests is commendable, Miss Jonas,' Meredith said. 'Worthy of a citation, at the very least. But we're not interested in pinching paper and pencils and rubber bands. Do you think you could forget your trust long enough to open these drawers and let us have a peek inside?'

Miss Jonas coloured. 'There's no call to be rude.'

'No, I suppose there isn't. But we'd appreciate it if you tried to think beyond the firm's nickels and dimes for a few minutes. We're investigating a murder. From the way the case is shaping up, we're going to have to probe pretty far below surfaces for the why of things. The reason we're here is to find out what Pauline Rourke's working life tells us about her. The way she did her housekeeping could tell us a lot, or it could tell us nothing. Are you going to unlock these drawers?'

A moment of hesitation, and then, with an apologetic 'Of course,' Miss Jonas took a ring of keys from the pocket of her suit jacket and unlocked the drawers of the desk. 'I can't unlock the files – they're really confidential.' That was apologetic, too, and the look she gave Meredith was apprehensive. When no objection was forthcoming, she sank into a chair with a sigh. 'I'm sorry. I didn't mean to be obstructive. I'm sorry Pauline's dead and I hope you catch her murderer and I'll do anything I can to help, naturally. It's frightening to think of her meeting such a dreadful death. Almost unbelievable. She was such an inoffensive sort of person.'

'So everyone tells us,' Meredith said, his eyes on the drawer he was rifling. 'Have you been with the firm as long as she was, Miss Jonas?'

'Longer. Almost twice as long, as a matter of fact. She was here nine years, I've been here seventeen. Worked myself up from the ranks. Pauline was brought in from outside to be Adrian Lefebvre's secretary. Not that I resented her for it. Well, maybe just for a little while at first, but I got over it fast. I could see she was a cracker-jack. Also, I shared an office with her – that was in the days before anybody around the place thought a partner's private secretary warranted a private office – and sharing an office when there's friction is simply impossible.'

'What's the firm going to do about a replacement?'

'A massive search, I shouldn't wonder. Up hill and down dale and all the way to the moon, if necessary. There's no one in the organization qualified to step into her shoes. I can vouch for that.'

Meredith looked at her quickly. 'How about you?'

'Me? God forbid!' Her fervour left no doubt of her sincerity. 'To you it probably sounds like a move upstairs because Lefebvre's the senior partner, but not as far as I'm concerned. Anyway, Mr Styles wouldn't part with me. We get along just fine. He's tractable. Lefebvre I wouldn't work for at double the salary, and it could easily come to that or somewhere near it, considering all the overtime. That's just the trouble. Pauline was literally at his beck and call – couldn't call her life her own. He thought nothing of telephoning her at midnight to give her dictation. Without any apology, naturally. He takes the line that God put other people on this earth to serve him.' Miss Jonas stopped. It was clear from her face that she was reviewing her frankness, deliberating whether to retreat or press on.

She pressed on. 'Pauline came to us from Arthur O'Toole. The name wouldn't mean a thing to you, probably. He was something of a boy wonder in his day – won a few really spectacular cases. Then he faded a little, but his reputation remained as solid as a reputation could be. That's when Pauline joined him. He was more or less a one-man band and didn't like to delegate responsibility. Except to his secretary, naturally, and Pauline pretty much ran things over there. It was a lot different here and she – ' A pause. 'You used the word robot before. Maybe it wasn't too extreme. Wind her up and she went. Always punctual. Never missed a day's work, as far as I know. I remember one time when she had to have a tooth extracted. Anybody else would have taken the day off, or at least part of the day. Not Pauline. She had it done during her lunch hour, came straight back to the office, and settled down to work. I didn't even know she'd been to the dentist until she took out the pad he'd put in her mouth to staunch the bleeding, wrapped the God-awful thing in Kleenex as calmly as if it were chewing gum, and dropped it into the wastebasket. I think I'll remember that as long as I live.'

Pauline Rourke's brother was assistant professor of Educational Psychology at a girls' college on Long Island. On the telephone, he had expressed his willingness to assist the police and his doubt that he would be able to do so. Now, receiving Meredith in a tiny, book-lined, incredibly crowded, incredibly untidy study, he apologized for the fact that classroom commitments had prevented his submitting to questioning any sooner. Tall and lanky, given to quick, fitful movements that looked like fidgeting even when they had purpose, Dennis Rourke had a thin, worn, almost febrile countenance, with eyes that were widely spaced and grey like his sister's, dark hair that was soft and feathery like his mother's, and a beak of a nose that seemed to be his own. He did not look happy, but neither did he look like a man prostrated with grief.

'Pauline wasn't an especially warm person, as my mother probably told you,' Rourke said, plunging into his discourse without preamble, like someone acutely aware of the value of time. 'We aren't a close-knit family. Pauline never really forgave Mom for marrying Johnnie. It was something straight out of *Hamlet*, allowing for the sexual variation. More things in heaven and earth than are dreamt of in your philosophy, Sigmund. Hey, that's not bad, is it? Must remember to slip it into a lecture.' A grin bared extremely crooked, extremely yellow teeth.

Meredith, who was far from expecting a parade of wit, was taken aback. It must have showed, for Dennis Rourke's face became solemn again: solemn and slightly defensive.

'Don't get the idea that I'm entirely devoid of fraternal feeling. I'm not.' The tone was defensive, too.

'It's too early to be getting any ideas, Mr Rourke. I'm not sure I'm entirely clear on what you mean by the allusion. Did your mother remarry too soon after your father's death to suit your sister?'

'Well, no. That's taking me up a bit too literally – the funeral baked meats and so forth. No. It was a good five years. And I can't honestly say it was the classical Electra thing with Pauline, or at least I never saw signs of it in her behaviour.' A rueful note in Rourke's voice suggested that this had been something of a disappointment to him. 'She was only seven when my father died. That's old enough for any number of complexes, but he was practically a stranger to her. He wasn't much of a family man. That's not a first-hand opinion because I wasn't even two when he died, but everybody says he was a remote sort of bird, completely wrapped up in his work. One of those medical types who really enjoys being routed out of the house at all hours of the night. He had a bit of dough and he was insured up to his eyebrows – left enough to make Mom comfortable for life – and we got along all right without him. What ticked Pauline off was Johnnie. He's a cab driver, he looks like a cab driver, he has the mentality of a cab driver. All he ever had going for him was looks, and he worked them for all he was worth. The poor man's Casanova. To do the guy justice, he stopped chasing altogether after he married Mom, and he's not a bad egg. But Pauline couldn't stand him. The thing that went against the grain for her was the kind of relationship he and Mom have – two animals rubbing up against each other in the dark to keep warm. Pauline never had much patience with weakness.' There was resentment, faint but distinct, in this last. Rourke, conscious of it, grimaced and resumed, with unwarranted belligerence, 'Don't get the idea – '

'I'm not getting any ideas, Mr Rourke,' Meredith cut in quietly. 'I told you it's too early for that. At this stage I'm merely going fishing.'

The warlike spirit was not appeased. 'You won't find anything relevant in this ancient family history, unless you're angling for a suggestion from me that either my mother or Johnnie had reason to kill Pauline. If any such thought is crossing your mind – '

'Nothing is crossing my mind, Mr Rourke,' Meredith cut in, again quietly. 'It's a blank sheet of paper right now. Suppose you put down the artillery and listen to me for a minute. There's nothing so far that says the reason for your sister's death is anything connected with the family. You don't seem like a clan addicted to churning up one another's passions. I get the impression you stay away from each other a lot. Also, money doesn't enter into it. Your mother, as you said, is comfortable for life, and you're pretty well fixed yourself, thanks to your wife's inheritance. Both of you are worth far more than your sister was. Her savings didn't amount to more than a few thousand.'

'That much? I would have pegged it in the hundreds.' Rourke exposed his crooked teeth again, fleetingly. 'You're thorough. But I guess you have to be. An obsession with the almighty buck isn't a family failing. We have others, but not that one, maybe because we never had any financial worries. Pauline's attitude towards money could stand a little explaining. She earned a damn good salary, as I'm sure you know, but she didn't salt it away. She spent it making herself comfortable, indulging herself while she still had a fair capacity for enjoyment. Her thinking was that she had a couple of decades ahead of her to acquire that nest egg for her old age. She said she didn't want to be like those poor wretches who stint themselves when they're young and then, the minute they stop pressing and sit back to relax, they get sick and – ' Rourke broke off. His face, suddenly ashen, contorted with agony. 'My God! Sometimes I think we must have built-in crystal balls. Pauline lived her life like somebody who knew she'd never be old. My God!' The grey eyes clouded over; their sight turned inward.

Meredith waited for the spasm of grief to pass. Genuine grief. Unmistakably genuine grief.

The wait was not long. Rourke's long, nicotine-stained fingers fumbled in the litter on his desk and found, impossible as it seemed to find anything, cigarettes. He lit one and dropped the match into a dusty ashtray. 'Not much point in these emotional outbursts, is there? Look, there's something I have to say. It's not often that I agree with my mother – far from it – but about this I'm with her one hundred per cent. There's no damn reason for anybody to want to kill Pauline. Her life was tidy and transparent and didn't impinge on anybody else's. I think my mother's idea that it might have been a mistake – a wrong number, so to speak – is something you shouldn't dismiss lightly.'

'I'll bear that in mind, Mr Rourke. For the present, I'd like to hear everything you can tell me about your sister's life. I gather that it may not be much. You've already made it clear that you weren't close.'

'No, we weren't. As you so aptly put it, the passions didn't get churned up. But then it would have been hard for anybody to feel passionate about Pauline. She was too independent. She couldn't have been more than sixteen when she turned her back on the Church – said she didn't want crutches, she could stand on her own two feet. And years before that she delegated herself surrogate mother for me because she didn't think Mom was responsible enough. Efficient, Pauline was. Brought me up right. Always reasonable. Never nagged. Never pushed. The most she'd ever do was put a hand on the helm to help me steer if I asked her to.'

'You really didn't like her much, did you?'

A shrug. 'Do you like the headmaster at boarding school? Do you like the head nurse in the hospital where you've gone to have an operation? When you're a captive – and a kid is always a captive – it's almost better to have something to resent. Maybe what bugged me was my mother's abdication from her role – she had Johnnie. As a maternal type, level-headed Pauline, who never lost her cool, was a washout. And knew it. You see I'm being frank with you.'

'I appreciate that, Mr Rourke. Can you tell me anything about your sister's recent activities? I don't suppose she treated you to any great confidences, but now and then she must have given you some inkling of what was looming up on the horizon.'

'She didn't.' Rourke looked a little sheepish. 'She assumed that her life held so little interest for me that talking about it would send me into the land of nod, and she was right. I don't cut much of a figure as – ' He broke off.

There was a sudden commotion outside the door: angry whispering at high velocity.

'Well, come in and get it off your chest,' Rourke called out sharply, then, lowering his voice, explained to Meredith, 'Mustn't let them repress things. Bad for them.'

The door flew open and two boys rushed into the room. They stopped in their tracks, excitement momentarily forgotten, to gawk at Meredith, who must surely have been one of the few people they had ever seen with hair as red as their own.

The younger boy, who looked about seven, recollected his purpose first. 'Mommy says Aunt Pauline has gone away. Gone where? Why didn't she tell me she was going away?'

'I told you she's stringing you, stoop,' the older boy said, with all the confident wisdom granted by three or four additional years of living. 'Aunt Pauline's dead.'

'Oh, dear!' Now a plump, flame-haired woman appeared in the doorway. 'I'm sorry, Dennis. I tried to – '

'Gone where?' the younger boy repeated. His face was very white.

Rourke waved his wife and the older boy out. 'Denny's telling you the truth, Roger,' he said gently. 'Your Aunt Pauline is dead. Your mother should have given it to you straight.'

For a moment, Roger stood still, as though he had not heard, as though he were still waiting for an answer.

Then he turned and raced from the room, slamming the door behind him.

'He'll get over it,' Rourke said confidently. 'He's gone to throw a few punches at the hate doll, so by dinner-time he'll probably be past the aggressive phase. It'll take a while for him to forget, though. He was crazy about Pauline. One of these fixations kids get. Started about a year ago, out of the blue. He's not a demonstrative kid, and Pauline didn't do anything to turn him on. He just woke up one morning head over heels in love.'

Eleven of the women who had been in the ladies' lavatory at Longfields when Pauline Rourke met her death responded to the newspaper appeal to get in touch with the police. As far as could be determined (circumstances had not appeared to warrant taking the names of witnesses and no one had done it), there had been three or four times that number on the scene, but people – even the most law-abiding people – are notoriously shy about involving themselves in police business. None the less, if the statements of the civic-spirited volunteers were a reliable guide to what the shrinking violets had to offer, that shyness would not handicap this particular investigation unduly, at least in the opinion of Sergeant Drake, a patient man, who put the eleven ladies through their paces. Four of them had been inside cubicles at the crucial moment, emerging in the midst of chaos. Of the remaining seven, six had observed nothing about any of the other women present, and the exception, a Barnard College sophomore, had observed to so little purpose ('I know I spotted something funny about the woman who got in line behind her – not funny ha-ha, funny peculiar, like a freak show – but for the life of me I can't remember what it was') that Drake, brought up in the belief that colleges existed to stretch the mind, wondered, not for the first time, what it was they did exist for these days.

Nor did the session with John Strazzera prove any more fruitful. The skeleton in his closet was, predictably, a woman (a buxom blonde half his age, Drake conjectured). He admitted her without too much prompting; he admitted as well Pauline Rourke's knowledge of her. 'She ran into us in this restaurant on 8th Street one time. I pretended I didn't know her from a hole in the wall. How could I introduce this grey-haired old maid as my stepdaughter, for Pete's sake? She pretended she didn't know me either. Glad not to have to admit the relationship, probably. I expected her to go running to her mother with the glad word, but she didn't. If she had, I would have heard about it PDQ, I can tell you. Happened months ago, and the couple of times I saw Pauline after that she looked down her nose at me. But that was nothing unusual. She's been looking down her nose at me from the time she was a kid.'

The anchorage for the iron gate was a pair of yellow brick posts, substantial enough for the imagination to conjure up a gatekeeper lurking in a concealed recess of one or the other. But no gatekeeper emerged from either as Meredith got out of his eight-year-old Citroën. The gate was not locked, possibly because a visitor was expected or possibly because the signpost in front of the gate ('Private Property. Keep Out. This Means YOU!') was considered a sufficient deterrent to trespassers.

The house, approached via a winding macadam road, stood amid shrubbery on a slight rise. It was a colonial house, somewhat rambling in structure, and the immaculate white board exterior was imposing against the greenery. At the end of the road, flagstones made a path to a very solid, very weathered oak door, which was opened by a butler who looked as though he, too, had seen many seasons come and go. He admitted Meredith to a vast entrance hall, designated a chair, one of a pair of relics of a distant past with tall, scrolled backs and wide, flat seats, then made a noiseless journey over the parquet to an arch and disappeared. Meredith examined the seat he had been offered and was unable to determine why it was deemed preferable to any of the half-dozen others in the hall. Possibly there was a system of rotation in operation to ensure that all the chairs got equal wear. He did not sit down.

Fortunately – for Meredith was allowed to cool his heels until he could feel frost nipping at them – the entrance hall was a miniature museum of antiquities. He was undisturbed in his contemplation of a suit of armour; of a grandfather clock; of a handsome leather and brass umbrella stand that might well have been a reformed spittoon; of a glass-fronted mahogany cabinet (locked) that housed a collection of rocks and stones indigenous to the area and exhaustively identified on little white cards. He had finished with the cabinet and was just beginning an inspection of the massive crystal chandelier when the butler returned and beckoned silently, as though summoning a petitioner to a royal audience.

Royalty received in a room that was (for royalty) relatively modest – an office, panelled and furnished in rosewood. The man seated in a huge black leather wing chair behind an impressive six feet of desk was spare and wiry and probably well below the middle height, yet far from being swallowed up by his perch, he dominated the room and everything in it. Sparse tufts of white hair crowned a thin, rather wizened face stamped with the look of unbending arrogance that is bred by generations of wealth and authority (the Ozymandias look, as Meredith, who had seen it many times, had baptized it). On the desk in front of him was a heavy, faceted glass half filled with rich amber liquid, and the aroma of fine old bourbon permeated the air.

Meredith, motioned to a chair, also of black leather, sat down and found the upholstery glove-soft but firm. He made a mental bet with an imaginary opponent that he would not be offered a drink, and won it.

'I trust this will not take long.' The voice, though dry and somewhat waspish with age, lacked none of the expected lordliness. 'We dine promptly at eight-fifteen.' A wrist watch was pointedly consulted.

'How long it takes depends on how much you can tell me about Pauline Rourke, Mr Lefebvre.'

'Not much, I assure you. I scarcely knew the woman.'

'She was your secretary for nine years.'

'Precisely. My secretary. Which means that my contact with her was limited to the office. Well – ' A change of tone that was virtually a dismounting from the high horse. 'That's not strictly accurate. She sometimes accompanied me to conferences and social functions, on occasions when I thought it necessary to have some sort of record of the proceedings. Miss Rourke had an excellent memory. Also, she has been a guest here a number of times, not infrequently for entire week-ends when the work load at the office has been particularly heavy. As a matter of fact, she was scheduled to come out this coming week-end. The load is formidably heavy at the moment.' Then, with a leap back into the saddle, 'I simply do not know how we're going to cope. Of all times for her to die!'

'Damned inconsiderate of her,' was the comment that rose to Meredith's lips. He suppressed it. 'She didn't choose to die,' came out instead. Mildly. But not mildly enough, judging from the scowl it provoked.

'I'm quite aware of that. Frankly, I find it difficult to credit the newspaper accounts of Miss Rourke's death. They're so lurid. But then the newspapers invariably exaggerate or distort or even invent when it's a question of building up a sensational story, don't they?'

'Sometimes. But not this time. Even the tabloids stuck to the facts this time. They're lurid enough.'

'I see.' A brief pause while this was digested. 'Well, I can scarcely accuse *you* of exaggeration, can I? Although I must say I still have difficulty believing it. Miss Rourke never struck me as the sort of person whose going hence might one day serve as the subject of a television spectacular. Frankly, it surprised me that she should have attracted so much notice from anyone. She was the most unobtrusive of persons.'

'That opinion may rank at the top of the poll, but somebody obviously didn't subscribe to it. We have to investigate all aspects of her life, Mr Lefebvre. Her work was a very large aspect. One possibility is that something connected with the job might have had unforeseen repercussions. A remote possibility, admittedly, but – '

'Non-existent. I am not Perry Mason.'

'I realize that. Still, any part of the legal machinery could involve matters that somebody might have a strong reason for wanting to keep hidden. Maybe Pauline Rourke inadvertently stumbled on something like that.

I'd like to request permission to examine your files.'

'Out of the question. I have obligations to my clients. My files are confidential and will remain confidential. Only a court order would induce me to open them for inspection. I very much doubt that you could obtain a court order without cause, and you have no cause.'

'You're not being very co-operative.'

'I see no reason why I should be. There's nothing in my files that concerns you. If you persist in pressing the matter, I will fight you every step of the way, with all the power and influence at my command. And I assure you –'

'All right, Mr Lefebvre. You've made your position clear. Let's go on to your impressions of Pauline Rourke. You undoubtedly saw more of her than anyone else did over the course of the nine years she worked for you, and you said she was a guest here frequently. How did she behave when she came out here?'

'What do you mean, how did she behave? Like any other guest, of course. She didn't smash up the furniture, if that's what you're driving at.' Asperity rang out, was negated by a wave of the hand. 'As I told you, she was the most unobtrusive of persons. She adapted herself to the routine here so well one scarcely knew she was about. Just as she did at the office. I am very much a creature of habit, Lieutenant. I would venture to say that the arrangement of my days has varied scarcely at all during the past thirty years. I insist on having things run smoothly and I will not tolerate obstruction or interference. If Miss Rourke had been a more self-assertive type, she would not have been my secretary, no matter how great her competence. Needless to say, she was extremely competent.'

'So is a computer. You make it sound as though there wasn't much to choose between Pauline Rourke and a computer, as far as you were concerned.'

'That's putting it rather crudely. You'll excuse me if I don't rise to the bait you're dangling.' Lefebvre's tone was neutral. He consulted his watch again.

Meredith ignored the hint. 'What about other members of your household? I find it hard to believe that Miss Rourke could have visited here without making some impression on somebody.'

'You are most – ' Lefebvre broke off (leaving Meredith in doubt as to which of many unpalatable qualities he possessed in such abundance). 'I'm aware that it's necessary for you to persist in your inquiries. It may be that my wife can be of some help to you. Possibly my daughter as well, but that's far less likely. Though she was acquainted with Miss Rourke, she has resided outside the country for the past five years and her memories of the acquaintance are not vivid. However, it is your duty to overturn every stone. Even pebbles.' The glass of bourbon was lifted and drained with an aplomb that the most confirmed bar-fly might have envied. 'They'll be in the drawing-room. It's virtually dinner-time, but I suppose dinner can be put back for a few minutes this once.'

An immense concession, clearly.

In this house, drawing-room was not a misnomer, not the appellation for a living-room with pretensions current in present-day usage. This drawing-room, with hanging tapestries and the contents of a successful pirate's treasure chest in gold fittings, possessed a grandeur that bespoke innumerable decades of receiving the great. To be able to take one's ease in such a room requires the habit of taking much for granted, and the three who sat nursing preprandial cocktails had the look of people who have taken any number of things for granted all their lives. The most commanding presence, and not only because a woman far advanced in pregnancy assumes an importance to take precedence over all challengers, was a statuesque woman, somewhat past her first youth, with a Grecian profile, a chignon like a knob of burnished mahogany, and a fine cleavage draped with smoky chiffon. Not much to Meredith's surprise, she was introduced first – Lefebvre's daughter, Elizabeth Sayres, present under the paternal roof for an extended stay to await the birth of her child. Her husband, Wallace Sayres, a Guatemalan businessman, was introduced next, with an intonation that implied he had an interest in all that country's businesses (and perhaps he had). He was as fine a physical specimen as his wife, tall, with broad shoulders tapering to a slim waist and no sign of flabbiness anywhere, though his leonine head of dark hair was grizzling and his face, taut and tanned and clear-eyed as it was, put him well on the wrong side of forty. But perhaps it was not the wrong side for a man whose looks in his younger days must have been the sort to kindle women and alienate men on sight, and even now relegated breeding and intelligence to a back seat. Mrs Lefebvre, last in the roll call but by no means negligible, had bestowed height upon her daughter and also the Grecian profile, in herself rendered stark by age and a coiffure that resembled sculptured silver. She had beautiful hands, the left adorned with a large, square-cut diamond; an even larger diamond ornamented the brooch at the throat of her black silk dress.

Three fairly impressive people, each of whom might

have dominated a gathering under other circumstances, and yet, the instant Adrian Lefebvre entered the room, he took it over. Meredith was mentally thrust back to grammar school and the memory of a female teacher not quite five feet tall, who had, on the first day of term, risen on the balls of her feet and regarded her charges in silence for an entire class period, cowing them into submission and holding the whip hand thereafter.

The trio, prompted by their tsar, were ready enough to trot out what they knew about Pauline Rourke. In the case of Wallace Sayres, the first to put his oar in, it turned out to be absolutely nothing. With a regretful shake of his head, he said, in a soft voice holding vestiges of an Australian accent, that he had never met her.

'You didn't miss much,' Elizabeth Sayres said with arrogant assurance, and the deference with which this pronunciamento was received by her husband made it abundantly clear who wore the pants in the Sayres household. 'Mousy little creature. All decent tailored suits of navy or charcoal and sensible shoes and efficient-looking handbags. And a personality to match.'

'Now, Elizabeth,' Mrs Lefebvre said mildly.

'I know that doesn't sound very gracious, Mother, but what's the point of going through the motions? A wet blanket is a wet blanket – it drips all over the carpet. It isn't as though we expected much of Pauline Rourke. She came here to work, after all. Still, she wasn't working every minute of the time. She could have managed to make herself agreeable instead of holing up in the library reading *Town and Country* when she couldn't escape to her room.'

'She seems to have made an impression on you, Mrs Sayres,' Meredith said. 'At least it sounds as though you observed her habits pretty closely.'

'I?' Elizabeth's eyebrows shot up. 'Good lord, no. I happened to find her in the library one day, that's all, and she behaved as though she wanted to crawl into the woodwork. No conversation at all, poor thing. Most of the time I hardly noticed she was about. I haven't set eyes on her for years and years. Certainly not since my marriage, which took place four years and ten months and thirteen days ago, to be exact.'

'And four hours,' Sayres murmured, and received from his wife, in return for this greater exactitude, a smile of dazzling radiance – dazzling, at any rate, to him, for he met it with an expression of adoration.

Meredith averted his eyes from the display of connubial felicity. 'What were your impressions of Pauline Rourke, Mrs Lefebvre?'

'Not very much different from my daughter's, to be honest. I was better acquainted with Pauline, of course. Over the years I've had any number of telephone conversations with her. Brief conversations – often no more than relaying a message from my husband – and hardly conducive to intimacy, but still, if there had been any warmth of personality I would have felt it. The first few times she visited us here I made efforts to draw her out, as any hostess would, but she resisted them.' Dejection softened the bony contours of Mrs Lefebvre's face momentarily. 'She preferred to be strictly professional where any of us were concerned. One had to respect that.'

'It hadn't occurred to me that preference entered into it,' Lefebvre snapped. 'It was simply a question of knowing her place.'

Mrs Lefebvre opened her lips, hesitated, and waved a hand vaguely, abandoning the field.

'That was poorly worded,' Lefebvre said, in a gentler tone. 'Lest you take me to mean that Miss Rourke dined with the servants, let me hasten to assure you that she came as a guest and was treated as a guest. But she never lost sight of the fact that she was an employee. She never presumed, and one could rely absolutely on her discretion. This coming Saturday is my birthday. Usually I celebrate it only with my nearest and dearest, but I had no hesitation about inviting Miss Rourke to make one of the family party.'

'And that is an honour and a half, to put it mildly,' Elizabeth said, with a playful little laugh. 'Daddy's just like a great big kid about his birthday. No outsiders need apply. And no insiders had better beg off. I remember trying to once. Did I get an earful!'

Adrian Lefebvre, autocrat of the breakfast, lunch, and dinner table, looked – wonder of wonders – distinctly embarrassed. 'It's an old man's fancy to make an occasion of having survived another year, and my family is good enough to humour that fancy.'

'Fancy? Ukase, you mean.' Elizabeth was revealing unexpected sprightliness. She smiled at her husband. 'The time I tried to beg off was just after I met you. I wanted to stay in Acapulco because I was afraid to be parted from you even for a minute. But do you think Daddy would listen to reason?'

'All's well that ends well,' Lefebvre said, with a chuckle. 'You got your man, Elizabeth. And I'm to get a grandchild.'

The word was magic, suddenly transforming Elizabeth into a queen. Both her male courtiers gazed at her with a tenderness that was almost fatuous. From the expression on her face, it was clear that she revelled in the homage. A gleam of mischief came into her eye. 'Salome!' she called out imperiously.

The cat who responded to the summons was a magnificent animal with black-tipped reddish-brown fur. Her progress across the room was stately, and her spring into Elizabeth's lap graceful. The landing was heavy. Elizabeth laughed delightedly; all the more delightedly when she saw her father wince and her husband blanch under his tan. 'My blessed angel,' she crooned, sweeping masterful, caressing hands over the cat's fur. 'How is my precious darling this evening? My most precious, precious, *precious* darling?'

A spasm of annoyance flitted over Mrs Lefebvre's face. Adrian Lefebvre was scowling fiercely. But the most fascinating exhibit was Wallace Sayres. His lips were moist and parted, and he watched the caressing hands with eyes that were hot, avid, worshipful, full of longing. Slowly, his wife's eyes came up from her lap to seek and find his, and hers held promise, a touch of mockery, and reciprocated passion.

All at once, the decorum dictated by the presence of a stranger seemed to go up in smoke as the whole family started talking simultaneously. Remonstrances from the prospective father and grandparents over such blatant disregard for the prospective child's prenatal welfare were pooh-poohed by the prospective mother, who none the less promised to be more careful. The hullabaloo was succeeded by a round of billing and cooing, then by a discussion of the prospective child's postnatal welfare, with emphasis on what kind of background made for a happy childhood. Sayres reminisced about his early years in the Australian outback (sounding, to Meredith's ears, like a boy's adventure story, but maybe life in the Australian outback was like that). Elizabeth plumped for the tropics (sounding like a brochure issued by the government of an emergent country to attract settlers, but maybe life in the tropics was like that – if you had money). Lefebvre said that whatever the claims for one paradise or another, no grandson of his would first see the light of day in a foreign country. The discussion ended there.

Meredith reintroduced the subject of Pauline Rourke. Lefebvre, whose irascibility had lessened appreciably (he made no further references to the putting back of dinner), loquaciously paraded every scrap of information about the dead woman in his possession, but when all was said, what it amounted to was that Pauline Rourke had been an admirable secretary, setting her employer a course of unvaryingly smooth sailing from the moment she took up her duties until the moment of her death.

A long trestle table with a top of boards stood against a wall of the kitchen, and on the boards papers of diverse shapes and sizes were spread out in numerous little heaps, as for an esoteric game of solitaire. Meredith sat reading at the midpoint of the table; near his elbow were an empty coffee mug, a pack of cigarettes, and an ashtray with an impressive cargo of butts, most of them smoked down to the last inch.

He struck a match, and at that instant a girl came into the kitchen. A wraparound robe of fine wool moulded her tall, slender figure, and the colour, a deep plum, was flattering to her pale complexion and the lustrous black coil of hair on top of her head. Her bare feet made faint sucking noises on the linoleum as she went to the stove.

'I thought you were asleep,' Meredith said, without looking up.

'I was.' She lit the flame under the tall porcelain coffee-pot standing on a back burner. 'I woke up alone. I didn't like it. I never do.'

'That's the most shameless remark I've heard since breakfast. Don't you ever bother to put up a front?'

'What for?'

'You've got me there. I think it has something to do with playing the game. Not letting the side down. Stuff like that.'

'Oh.' She came to the table, picked up the ashtray and the mug, and carried them to the sink, emptying the one into the garbage can below and then rinsing the other under the tap. She replaced the ashtray on the table and went to stand in front of the stove, challenging the maxim that a watched pot never boils. 'Do you want something to eat? So you can keep up your battle strength.'

'There was some ham in the refrigerator. I ate that.'

Silence. Meredith finished with a paper and shoved it underneath the heap in front of him. He continued reading. In a moment, a sizzling noise from the coffee-pot. The girl shut off the gas, poured coffee into two mugs, and brought them to the table, setting one down at Meredith's elbow.

'Thanks, baby,' he said, still not looking up.

She sat down at the end of the table, holding her mug in both hands, blowing gently on the contents. Her eyes, deep-set and velvety black, the outstanding feature in a face a shade too angular and uncompromising to be termed beautiful, were pensive as they studied his grim profile. 'Still in the dark?'

'Not a glimmer of light. I'm beginning to doubt there ever will be. It should never have happened. She wasn't standing between anybody and a fortune. She wasn't trying to steal anybody's husband. She wasn't making a pain in the ass of herself to anybody. What else is there?'

'Maybe she got herself involved in something unsavoury and you just haven't found out about it yet. Or maybe the fact that she was so very, very ordinary was camouflage and she was really – '

'An undercover agent for the Martians.'

She laughed. 'Well, you did ask. Sort of.'

'I did.' He met her eyes, and some of the grimness left his face. 'It won't turn out to be anything like that. I'll be ready to eat my badge if it does. She was the most innocuous specimen ever to pop out of the womb. No dark corners in her life. Everything is here.' His hand cut a swath in air over the table. 'A real pack rat. She kept bills and cancelled cheques and documents that go back to the year one. Snapshots of everybody she ever knew. Letters she received when she was in her teens. If it's all a smoke screen, she must have spent a hell of a lot of time rubbing sticks together.' He gulped down his coffee and resumed reading. 'Go back to bed, Cassandra. There's no need for both of us to sit up with the patient.'

'I've been thinking.' She sipped her coffee slowly, her eyes never leaving his face. 'About Pauline Rourke. You're not the only one who has her on the brain.'

'That sounds ominous. I'd worry about it if I believed it. You said you were asleep.'

'They say you can think in your sleep. But I meant off and on since yesterday. That living-room of hers has been haunting me.'

'Why?' He looked at her quickly. 'I thought you liked it.'

'I did. I loved it. I don't think I've ever seen a more beautiful room. When I was there, I felt I'd almost be willing to sell my soul to live in a room like that. But afterwards – ' Cassandra finished her coffee and put down the empty mug – 'I started wondering about the why of it. The need it answered, I mean. Not one of the simple ones. You said she didn't entertain, so she wasn't putting on a display to garner tributes from other people. She didn't run with a pack of collectors, which would have put the hunting on a social basis, more or less. But there was a need, and obviously it must have been a strong one. I've been thinking about it, and what I've come up with – Do you remember that lovely Queen Anne settee I was so mad to buy a couple of months ago?'

'Yes.'

'You said sure it was lovely, but what were we going to do with it except look at it? As soon as you said that, I realized you were right and I didn't want it any more. But a year or so ago, if I'd had a chance at a bargain like that, I'd have snapped it up and gone full tilt at the job of building a room around it. And the whole business would have been out of proportion, a demand for things to give me more than they should be asked to give. Pauline Rourke's apartment strikes me as answering just such a demand. Everything's so schematic. The living-room. The kitchen with every kind of culinary gadget that's ever been invented. That stage set of a bedroom. Even her wardrobe. She must have tracked down fabrics and accessories the way she tracked down furniture. Most women own a few articles of clothing that go against type, even if they're not impulse buyers. She didn't. She planned everything down to the last pair of stockings. All in all, I get an impression that perhaps she was burrowing in for the millennium. Building a kind of bomb shelter around herself. Does that make sense?'

'It makes plenty of sense, but whether it adds up to anything useful – ' Meredith shrugged. 'Could be there was some trauma at some time or other and she was cushioning herself against further bombardment. If there was, we'll find out about it. The thing is, it doesn't sound like a reason for murder.'

'No, it doesn't. Just the other way. Concentrating so hard on things suggests that she'd gone off people, and things don't commit murders.'

'That's a brilliant conclusion, baby. Makes out a real case for thinking in your sleep.'

'I'm glad you like it. Perhaps we could put a tape recorder beside the bed. Then you won't miss out in the event that anything comparable gets voiced.'

Meredith laughed. 'It's tempting, but sometimes duty has to be sacrificed to decency. Go back to bed. And try to give the little grey cells a rest, so you don't wake up with a brain fever. '

'You're a fine one to talk.' Cassandra rose and carried the empty mugs to the sink, rinsed them under the tap and placed them on the draining rack. Then she returned to the table and bent to kiss Meredith's forehead. Her robe parted, baring her breasts.

He drew the lapels together.

'Oh, my. You're really in a bad way, aren't you?'

He reached for her hand and brought it to his lips. When he released it, she rested it on the top of his head for an instant.

'Don't sit up all night, Mike.' And then she was gone.

Meredith went back to his reading.

DATA FOR THE COMPUTER/GRIST FOR THE MILL

Thick, green, evenly trimmed grass, bisected by a concrete path on either side of which slippery elm and white oak stand at regular intervals, like sentries. The path leads to a four-story red brick building that proclaims institution (it houses the Amsterdam College library and the offices of the English Department). Pedestrian traffic, very brisk, is largely a promenade of females; at the moments when there is no male in view, the atmosphere is distinctly cloistral.

Beneath a tree a girl sits cross-legged with a textbook open across her thighs, facing away from the path, her back against the trunk but clearly not in need of support. Her austere costume of man-tailored white shirt and Black Watch plaid skirt, white socks and black loafers suggests a uniform, but the dress of the pedestrians evincing no regimentation, one must deduce choice. She does not strike the eye as a particularly attractive girl, even though the parts, taken one by one, are more than acceptable. Torso: slender, almost hipless, with small, rounded breasts. Legs: slim and shapely. Hands: capable-looking, with square palms, spatulate fingers, and short, buffed nails. Hair: dark brown and healthy, cropped in a style that requires little attention. Face: heart-shaped, with high forehead, widely-spaced grey eyes slightly dimmed by glasses with heavy black frames, straight nose, sharply defined mouth perhaps a fraction too small. All this adds up to the adolescent Pauline Rourke.

Someone swerves from the path and approaches the tree. She is a tall, robust girl, walking with an athletic bounce that sets her blonde pony tail bobbing jauntily. But there is nothing jaunty about her face – pale and drawn and tense, with a telltale redness around limpid blue eyes never destined for sorrow. With an ease that again betrays the athlete, she squats opposite Pauline, who looks up quickly, startled. For a moment, they gaze at each other in silence, and then, as tears start in the blue eyes, Pauline looks down again and goes on with her reading; turns a page, progressing from the embryo of a frog to the foetus.

The blonde girl wipes her eyes with a stiff hand. 'You saw,' she says dully. 'I suppose that's what the look you gave me meant.'

'Yes,' Pauline murmurs, to her book.

'Well, what are you going to do about it?' A defiance that carries no conviction.

'That depends on what you do. You know that.'

'What if I don't do anything?'

'Then there's only one thing I can do.' Pauline closes her book and meets the blonde girl's eyes. Her own hold determination, yet there is compassion in them as well. 'You know that, too.'

'Of all the breaks. Of all the lousy, rotten, stinking breaks. Other people get away with it all the time, but the first time I try – ' The blonde girl's voice falters. 'It's not fair. It's just not fair. With all the zombies on campus who are deaf, dumb, and blind, why did I have to be sitting next to you?'

It is not a question that seems to expect an answer. Pauline makes none.

'It really was the first time, you know.' A plea in the voice; a plea in the blue eyes. 'The very first time, I swear to God. I was out on the court practising my backhand till all hours last night and by the time I called it quits I was so pooped I – Well, I just couldn't memorize the lousy dates. What's the point of memorizing them anyway? Old Flathead Fielding is always telling us that concepts are what really matters, and then he keeps us up all night before exams memorizing stuff we'll forget the very next day!'

The compassion in Pauline's eyes deepens, but there is no lessening of determination.

'Okay, I'm rationalizing. I know it. You don't have to get all holier-than-thou.' The blue eyes fill with tears. 'Cheating is cheating. There's no justification. I can't even claim I succumbed in a moment of real bleak terror. It was deliberate. I marked that handkerchief with the intention of carrying it into the classroom. Oh, I kidded myself a little – told myself that maybe a miracle would happen and I wouldn't have to use it, but – ' A shrug. 'Go ahead and report me.'

'I don't want to report you.'

'Well, nobody's twisting your arm!'

'I don't want to report you,' Pauline repeats, very quietly. 'I'm glad you sought me out to talk things over. If you hadn't, I would have sought you out. There's an alternative to my reporting you. You know that as well as I do. A much better – '

'Fat chance! Forget it!'

'Listen to me for a moment.' Pauline's voice, though still quiet, is urgent; she leans forward, gripping her ankles. 'I wish I hadn't seen the handkerchief. Honestly. But I did see it. That's past remedy. Having seen it, I'm on my honour to report it. But there's someone whose honour is more deeply concerned than mine, and that's you. If you report yourself, it would make things easier all around.'

'Easier for you, you mean. I can just see myself walking into Honour Court and telling the president I'm there to 'fess up because if I don't Pauline Rourke will do it for me. No, thanks. I'll pass up that moment of glory.'

'There's no need to tell it that way. Why bring me into it at all? Just tell her what happened. You yielded to temptation when the pressure got heavy and you regretted it later because you're an honourable person. Which is no more than the truth. Even if I hadn't seen you, your conscience would never have given you a moment's peace. I know it. I'm sure of it.' And indeed, Pauline's eyes are alight with absolute conviction. 'Report yourself. It's the best way. You won't regret it, I promise you.'

. . . *It's the weirdest thing, but I can see it all now as clearly as if it happened yesterday. Funny how some things stay with you, isn't it? It was spring, I remember, and the day was unusually warm. I even remember the quality of the light – that late afternoon glow you think wouldn't have a chance to get through the clouds, but somehow it does. Before that little heart-to-heart, I hardly knew Pauline Rourke. She was just another member of the freshman class to me. The kind with a reputation for being goody-goody, and I fancied myself a real daredevil. I wasn't, of course. I was all kinds of a coward. My God, the effort it took to nerve myself up to having it out with her! I stood at the library window for about half an hour before I could manage it, and the sight of her sitting there on the grass so remote and calm and sure of herself – Well, she really went to work on me with her little sales pitch, hammering away until I was ready to agree to anything. And you know, she was right. I really did feel better afterwards. The punishment was no great shakes. A stiff lecture from the Dean was the worst of it. Also, I was tapped for the job of counselling other girls who yielded to temptation – sort of like a cured member of Alcoholics Anonymous preaching the gospel. By all that's right, they should have made me drop out of the tennis tournament, but they didn't, probably because they didn't want to miss a chance to have good old Amsterdam make a showing. Not that I could do much against a Radcliffe girl with a service there ought to be a law against, but I did get to the semi-finals, which is further than any – I'm rambling. Excuse me. Pauline kept her mouth shut about the whole business, of course. Never even mentioned it to me again. I felt I owed her a lot. In fact, I sort of considered her my guardian angel and ran to her with all my troubles. Not that we were ever all that close, but we did correspond for a while after college, when I was touring the tennis circuit and feeling homesick and – You mean she kept those letters? My God! They were nothing but gripes and – No, I don't have any of hers. The correspondence fizzled out after a while. In recent years we've exchanged Christmas cards and that's about it. And she sends birthday cards for the kids. She never forgets. Forgot, I mean. What an awful thing. No, I can't think of a single reason why anybody'd want to kill her. But then I haven't seen her in ages. People change . . .*

A bedroom. At a window, curtains are parted on a vista of moon-drenched snow. In the fireplace, a fire is dying. An occasional crackle of wood is the only sound; an occasional flicker of flame the only movement. The bed is large, and there are two people in it. One is Pauline Rourke, who lies on her side, her bare arm outside the patchwork quilt. She is gazing into the fire, and by its glow her youthful face looks soft and dreamy and vulnerable. The man who shares the bed is considerably older, at least twice Pauline's age and possibly more, with a much wrinkled, weatherbeaten face and iron-grey hair growing low on his forehead and high on his cheeks in a bristly beard that appears a barrier to human contact. He lies on his back, smoking, and the pungent aroma of black tobacco is strong in the air. His free hand is entwined with Pauline's.

'You'll have to be going soon,' he says. His voice is deep and gruff and the intonations are unmistakably English.

'I suppose so.'

'You don't seem concerned about the risk. But then you never are. How I envy you. Not yet twenty, and so self-possessed.' He releases Pauline's hand, throws off the quilt, and begins to stroke her back slowly, all along its length. 'At your age I felt hopelessly inadequate to everything. An uncooked suet pudding.'

Pauline says nothing. She smiles at the fire.

'I can hear what you're thinking, doubting Thomasina.' He pinched her buttocks, none too gently. 'And you're right, of course. There was the work. By the time I was sixteen I was as committed a little bugger as you'd find anywhere. And I've never looked back.'

'No reason why you should have.'

'None. Unfortunately, I've never looked right or left either, only straight ahead. Which sometimes makes life difficult for other people.'

Pauline stirs, attempts to roll over to face him, but meets resistance in the hand that exerts pressure against the small of her back.

'I can hear that, too. Don't bother to say it.' He crushes out his cigarette in the ashtray on the bedside table. Then he rolls over on his side and draws her to him, her back against his front. He begins to rub her stomach with a slow, regular, almost hypnotic motion.

The only sound in the room is the crackling of embers in the fireplace. The two in the bed appear to be listening to it, or to something beyond it. Again Pauline tries to turn around; again he prevents her.

'I have so little to give you,' he murmurs against her hair, his breath sending the short tendrils every which way. 'And the young need so much, don't they? So very, very much.'

This time Pauline's effort to turn is determined, and opposition gives way. She slides her arms around his neck and kisses him ardently. It is a lengthy kiss, and during the course of it the initiative passes to him. Once in command, he gathers momentum like a locomotive going downhill. His love-making is vigorous and proceeds towards self-gratification without pauses at checkpoints to see if his companion is with him. But she is.

Afterwards, they both lie on their backs under the quilt without touching, their eyes on the ceiling. Once again they seem to be listening, but now there is scarcely anything to hear, the almost extinguished fire crackling at longer and longer intervals. Moments pass. He lights a cigarette.

'I always feel now as though the waters are closing over my head,' Pauline murmurs.

He makes no comment. Possibly he has not heard, for

the countenance he offers the ceiling is blank and closed, as though the intelligence behind it were miles away.

Pauline rolls over and faces the fire again, or, rather, the memory of a fire: extinction is total now. 'For the longest time there was nothing. Absolutely nothing. I used to feel like a sack of potatoes, lying there and wishing in my heart of hearts that the whole thing would be over quickly. I often wondered how you stood it. And then all of a sudden the wall insulating my senses simply disintegrated. I couldn't believe it. I couldn't believe things were really happening to me. I'd always assumed nothing ever would, you see.'

'For the longest time.' His mimicry of her tone is half playful, half sorrowful. 'My dear child, you're so young. Much too young for these sexual worries. But I suppose you wouldn't be a proper American if you didn't have them. In this country, the demons aren't under the bed, they're in it. For women, it's frigidity. For men, it's homosexuality. It's a wonder to me how you manage to carry on the breed in spite of it all.'

Pauline laughs. The sound is quickly engulfed by the silence. With the fire dead, the fireplace is no more than an obscure, uninteresting shape in the murk, but she continues to gaze at it.

'I'm glad I can give you that,' he says quietly. 'It's about the only thing I *can* give you, God knows. Don't bother to deny it. I shan't believe you.'

She takes him at his word and holds her peace. Her face discloses that whatever the gift is, it is enough. He cannot read the message, but he seems to receive it some other way, and he gives her shoulder an affectionate pat.

Moments pass. Moments during which he crushes out one cigarette, lights another.

Presently Pauline gives a soft, regretful sigh. 'I really should be going, I suppose.'

'Umm,' he assents absently.

She rolls over to look at him, sees that he has gone away from her, props herself up on her elbow to wait. It is a lengthy wait – almost to the end of his cigarette.

'Pauline.' He utters her name tenderly, caressing her with it. 'About that second demonstration for the Intermediate Lab. You know, I'm not satisfied that I've made it quite as clear as it might be.'

Pauline smiles. Without haste, she folds back the quilt and climbs out of bed. The lamp on the bedside table clicks on as she glides from the room. She returns almost at once with notebook and pencil in hand, not quite so naked as before: she is wearing her glasses.

. . . virtually impossible to state unequivocally what Pauline Rourke meant to me. Quite apart from the dulling of sensibility caused by the passage of time, I am much too aware that I write all this to a total stranger whose interest in her is necessarily limited to how and why she came to make her final appearance above ground in the police mortuary. None the less it is essential to do one's best. I was extremely fond of Pauline, and my memory of the affair leaves a warm glow over terrain that is largely tundra. I cannot boast that my behaviour was such as to cover me with glory. It started as a simple, straightforward seduction. Quite callous and cold-blooded. I was a stranger to your shores, living alone, feeling I needed a woman, and I took advantage of the admiration I inspired in one of my students. Quite apart from being the best of a dreary lot, Pauline was my laboratory assistant, consequently convenient. In fact, it was on the floor of the laboratory that I had her for the

first time. Once over the shock, she proved a most willing partner. Americans as a race, I've discovered, are tremendously one-sided. With Pauline it took the form of work worship: 'THE COMMITTED CAN DO NO WRONG' (capitals are essential). I wasn't the first, or at least she said I wasn't the first. It occurs to me now that she might have denied me the credit for despoiling her virginity to spare me guilt pangs. (As though one could feel guilt over something so inconsequential. As though one had the time. But apparently one can and one has – in America.) Possibly she was telling the truth. She never told me who my predecessor had been. No one of any competence, clearly. I always harboured the notion that Pauline had helped some sensitive young adolescent 'find himself' (in the language of your country) by offering her lily-white body. The quixotic, slightly addled approach to sex: that was her line. I found it charming. It demanded so little. The lily-white body was nothing to be sneezed at either. A bit on the scrawny side, but perfectly proportioned, and one had the sense that the flesh was melting under one's touch.

The year I spent as exchange professor at Amsterdam College was one of the most delightful of my life, largely because of Pauline. But of course it had to end. It was necessary ultimately to return. One had one's obligations. One's work. One's family. Pauline knew from the beginning that it was a liaison without a future and was adult enough to accept that. She wasn't the sort to weave fantasies out of dust. None the less the parting was painful. Not that she failed to behave well. She behaved splendidly, perfectly splendidly. I was the one who went to pieces: I must have added a gallon or two of salt water to the ocean on the voyage home. Shameful, but there you are. Reflecting on what I was leaving behind and what I was returning to would have drawn tears from a stone, but there's no point in expatiating on that. I'm sure you're not concerned with my marital history.

I cannot pretend to be desolated with grief. Over the years, Pauline and I have rather lost touch (how apt that expression: touch is what one loses when it is no longer possible to touch). However, even a confirmed egotist can cherish memories, and I hope you will believe that my expression of regret over Pauline's death is something more than a formality. I am appalled at so vile and furtive a mode of execution, and I find it difficult to believe that she could have done anything to merit it. Indeed, I cannot help wondering whether, in fact, she intercepted a fate meant for someone else, but that, presumably, you are in a better position to judge than I. Should there be anything further I can do to assist your inquiries, I am at your disposal.

Yours sincerely . . .

A bedroom, dazzlingly illuminated by a strong overhead light and a couple of lamps. Two large, barred windows let in the night, more light from the building across the street, and doubtless the gaze of any voyeurs who inhabit that building. The furniture is fairly standard dormitory issue: single bedstead; desk and chair; tallboy; bookcase; two arm-chairs with lumpy upholstery and sagging springs. Superimposed on these bare bones are a plenitude of rugs, cushions, hangings, afghans, and scarves in brilliantly coloured, lavish fabrics, many of which are faded and threadbare – trappings suitable to the harem of a sultan who has seen better days, an observer with a high sense of the ridiculous might conclude. Nothing about three of the room's four occupants, who lounge in negligees like odalisques – one leafing through *Vogue*, another cutting articles from back issues of *Theatre Arts*, the third painting her fingernails each in a different shade of polish – contradicts that conclusion. The fourth person in the room is Pauline Rourke, who sits at the desk in a dove grey blouse and a darker grey pleated skirt, with her thick-rimmed glasses perched on her nose, hemming a serviceable-looking beige tweed skirt, and who seems thoroughly out of place, unless (to push the fantasy to its limit) one supposes her on the scene to take charge of the sultan's offspring.

The phonograph on top of the bookcase, wherein a small collection of books (mainly texts) is crowded on one shelf while the rest of the space is allotted to records, emits the passionate *andante con moto* of Schubert's E-flat piano trio. Pauline is listening. Possibly the slim, long-legged girl with hair of a magnificent dark auburn that no chemicals have ever approximated is listening, too, as she reclines on the bed with *Vogue*. The others clearly are not. When the movement concludes and the turntable shuts itself off with a click, the *Vogue* reader (whose room it is) stirs lazily, but it is Pauline who gets up to turn the record over and start the turntable again.

The *scherzo* wends its brief way with zest; without disturbing any of the activities. Then, during the pause before the start of the concluding *allegro moderato*, the auburn-haired girl yawns aloud and says, 'I'm hungry.' She might be described as beautiful were it not for a too-wide mouth with a sullen droop that bodes no good for anyone who crosses her.

Pauline glances up from her sewing and meets the auburn-haired girl's eyes with a smile.

'I'm hungry.' The repetition is mouthed silently.

'In a few minutes,' Pauline mouths back. She gestures at the phonograph and bends over her sewing again.

The sullen mouth becomes taut, opens for speech. But the words are suppressed. *Vogue* is closed gently. The auburn-haired girl closes her eyes and gives herself up to the music.

The other two odalisques are hungry, too, they announce when the record is over. Three cheeseburgers are requested. Pauline nods and stuffs her sewing into a straw basket.

'I've changed my mind,' the auburn-haired girl says. 'Make it ham and Swiss on rye instead. And a chocolate ice-cream soda with chocolate ice-cream. Please specify chocolate ice-cream, Pauline.' This is almost plaintive. 'Don't let them put in vanilla again.'

'I always do specify,' Pauline says. 'I can't see what they're doing behind the counter, though.'

'You could lean over.' This from the nail polisher, a would-be *femme fatale* whose natural black hair is adorned with zebra stripes of bleach.

'Or climb up on it.' From the *Theatre Arts* fan, who wears her light brown hair loose except for two narrow braids at the temples: a cue to enter strewing rosemary and rue would find her ready. 'That ought to get results.'

'Or an ambulance,' Pauline says, with a laugh, and looks at the auburn-haired girl.

No advice is forthcoming from this quarter. The auburn-haired girl is writing on a pad. She finishes and rips off the top sheet. 'Hand them this.' She tosses the paper towards the desk. It lands on the floor.

Pauline picks it up and looks at it. *This girl is deaf and dumb. Please follow instructions exactly. One ham and*

Swiss on rye – NO MUSTARD!!! One chocolate ice-cream soda with chocolate ice-cream – NOT VANILLA!!!! Pauline's face shows nothing. Calmly, she crumples the paper, throws it into the wastebasket beneath the desk, and gets to her feet.

'Get me a chocolate malt,' the *Theatre Arts* fan says, when Pauline is almost at the door.

Pauline stops, glances inquiringly at the nail polisher, who starts to shake her head, then looks pensively down at her rather wide hips and shrugs.

'Aw, what the hell. Ditto.' A melodramatic sigh. 'My God, it's a bore being campused. What good does it do to confine us to the dormitory in the evenings, I'd like to know? I have to cut so many classes to see Jerry I'm flunking everything. I sure wish there was some way of getting in and out of this fortress besides the front door.'

Pauline, who has reached the door, stops again, looks again at the nail polisher. 'Try the laundry-room window on the far right. Two of the bars are loose and lift out. Anybody but a tub can get through the opening.'

The reaction is incredulity in triplicate: three pairs of popping eyes, three gaping mouths. But it is lost on Pauline, who does not linger to see it.

. . . knocked us over with a feather when she came out with that one. If I'd ever drawn up a list of people who might be in the know about escape routes, Pauline Rourke would have been the last one on it. Well, of course she was giving us the straight dope. Why else would I remember it? The three of us gave that window a pretty good work-out the rest of the year, let me tell you. Why did Pauline Rourke hang around a dissolute trio like us? I know you didn't phrase the question that way, but it's what you meant, isn't it? Of course I'm not

insulted. We were a pretty raunchy bunch, I have to admit. Nobody liked us much. We didn't like ourselves much. I don't suppose Pauline liked us much either, as a bunch. She liked me all right, though. We were in the same music appreciation class in the first half of our junior year, and we were about the only ones who really listened. I've always been addicted to music. Studied the piano as a kid. Didn't get very far with it, but far enough to get hooked. I've never understood how people can live without music. They can, though. If you love it the way I do, you sometimes feel you're all alone in the stratosphere. Except for prissy music majors and poseurs, and who the hell wants them? I wouldn't say Pauline was all that musical, but her responses were genuine. She appreciated having access to my records, and in return she didn't mind doing favours. A kind of quid pro quo, *you might say. Or maybe she would have done them anyway. I can't answer for her motives. Hell, I can't even answer for my own. We got along, that's all. We were never buddies, though, and I'm wondering how you happened to get my name. I haven't given Pauline Rourke a thought in years. In fact, when you telephoned, for a minute I couldn't even remember who – Letters? What letters? Oh, yes, I remember now. The one I wrote her when I decided not to come back to college for senior year. I decided to get married instead. You should have seen the tract she sent by return mail! Words of wisdom about how I shouldn't throw myself away before I developed my potential, etcetera, etcetera. The president of Amsterdam couldn't have done a better job of ladling out the bullshit. Maybe I'm being unfair. Maybe she thought anybody I'd latch on to at that stage of my life would be a dud as a husband. He was. The three who came after him were duds, too. Fancy her keeping that letter all these years. A little pitiful, when you think about it. What else can I tell you about her? Let me see. There was gossip about her being mixed up with some faculty member during her sophomore year, but I never believed it. Zoology professor. An Englishman. Strictly the orang-outang type. A beard like barbed wire, and he reeked so of tobacco you couldn't get within ten yards of him without your knees buckling. To say nothing of the fact that Pauline was such an uptight little – Still, she did have the word on that laundry-room window. You never know about people, do you? . . .*

A large boudoir. The ivory carpeting is as thick and soft as a fox's pelt. The ivory walls are quilted with satin, except one, which is all sliding doors, some of them open on a lavish display of women's clothes. There are a chaise-longue and chairs of ivory brocade and a kidney-shaped dressing-table of intricately carved white wood polished to an illusion of translucency and adorned with gold fittings. On the dressing-table is a magnificent gold-framed three-way mirror, reflecting myriad images of a young woman who sits very erect in ivory satin lounging pyjamas and watches herself wield a mother-of-pearl brush over her long, straight, gleaming dark hair. Hers is a handsome face rather than a beautiful one – long and narrow, with widely spaced dark eyes accented by thick, arched brows, jutting cheek bones, aquiline nose, mouth that might have been the work of a sculptor's chisel. It is a face that takes getting its own way as a matter of course. It is the face of the young Ivy Eastbrook, as public as the face of a movie star.

Pauline Rourke sits on the edge of the chaise-longue

like someone waiting for a train, and her tailored black dress with demure white collar would induce even those who do not pride themselves on their perception to hazard a guess as to what kind of traveller she would be. Her face is pale and set and angry. Her eyes seek Ivy's in the mirror, but without success.

'You're out of your mind,' Pauline says. 'You are absolutely out of your mind. Stark, staring mad.'

There is a tremor of the sculptured lower lip in the mirror, but the portended outburst does not occur. The tempo of the brushing accelerates slightly.

'You'll never be able to rely on him,' Pauline goes on. 'He has no backbone. He's a jellyfish, not a man. You have sharp elbows, Ivy. You'll give him a shove, and you won't meet any resistance or break any bones. He'll simply go "squish" and slide away from you. You'll never be able to stand it.'

For a moment, Ivy does not react. Then the guarded mask in the mirror dissolves in a disarming grin. 'You paint a graphic picture, I have to admit.' Ivy puts down the brush and meets Pauline's gaze in the mirror. 'You don't have to tell me he's weak. I'm not deluding myself he's any tower of strength. That far gone I'm not. But what does it matter? I'm strong enough for ten.'

'I know it. That's just the trouble. It never works, this reversal of the sexual roles.' Now it is Pauline's eyes that become elusive and drop to her hands, which are folded in her lap like a schoolgirl's. 'I don't know what you see in him to make the prospect of having him around all the time appealing. The physical attraction I can understand. He's good-looking enough to hang up on the wall, God knows. But why marry him? It's not as though you've ever given a hoot about being conventional.'

'Of course not. And I never will.' Ivy props her elbows on the dressing-table and cradles her chin in her hands. She is smiling at herself now, a bit wistfully. 'But he does. He's such a sweet, simple soul in some ways. A stickler for the proprieties. All tender concern for my honour. Can you imagine? He won't come here except to call for me or bring me home. Our little love nest is so well under cover I feel like Mata Hari every time we have a rendezvous. I keep telling him I have no honour to lose, but it doesn't seem to have any effect. For him a lady's a lady, no matter what she might have done. Old-fashioned chivalry like that kind of gets to you after a while.'

'So does the tsetse fly, if you don't take precautions. Oh, Ivy!' Sorrow, Reproach. Exasperation. 'I never thought I'd live to hear anything so fatuous from you. Haven't you even considered the possibility that he might be piling it on? It's the first thought that would occur to anyone else. I assure you. He's so transparent. A lap dog sniffing around for a berth.'

Ivy's face goes hard. 'If you're trying to tell me he's interested in my money, save your breath. Who the hell isn't?'

'I'm not saying it's as simple as that. Probably he's not only deceiving you, he's deceiving himself as well. Probably – '

'What have you been doing, dipping into your kid brother's psychology textbooks?'

'Not for the likes of Geoffrey Cheyney. He's too elementary a case. You're the one who's worth study.'

'Listen, Pauline – '

'No, you listen to me!' Pauline's eyes are hot, and they rivet Ivy's in the mirror. 'I can see now what it is that gets to you. It's not the gentlemanly bearing in itself, it's the fact that it comes attached to an ancestry that goes back to the Mayflower or the very next boat to make the trip. All that blue blood down on its knees before Ivy Eastbrook, whose father started out as – '

'I don't need a discourse on breeding from a third-generation refugee from the potato famine!'

'Fourth. Not that it should matter to anybody with any sense how far back the ascent from the ranks of the great unwashed took place. But obviously it matters to you. Just how did Geoffrey cast the spell, Ivy? Did he tell you how his forefathers taught the redskins to eat with a knife and fork?'

'Drop it, Pauline!'

'No, I won't drop it.' Pauline's passion has waned; her voice has the quietness of despair. 'For somebody else it might work. But not for you. A couple of months of being closed in with him and you'll be crawling up the wall. I hope for your sake it's only the money he wants. I hope for your sake he cleans out the cookie jar and takes himself off to – '

The mother-of-pearl hairbrush strikes Pauline's temple and rebounds to the carpet with a thud. Shock flits across her face, then gives way to a stony calm. Without a word, she picks up the brush and sets it on the chaise-longue, gets up and goes from the room.

. . . and that's about all there was to it. Pauline was hardly the type to take having things flung at her in stride. I could probably have smoothed it over with an apology, but I've never been good at apologizing. Anyway, I was too angry. She really touched a nerve – came down hard on what amounted to an obsession in those days. I minded like hell that these silver-spoon, born-to-

the-purple types I could have bought and sold a hundred times over felt they could high-hat me. Geoffrey Cheyney seemed like the answer to a prayer I didn't even know I'd uttered. Last scion of an old New England family, handsome, charming, and he really cared. What could be better? Penniless, of course, but what was that to me? I'd made up my mind that it would work. I couldn't forgive Pauline for playing the oracle, still less when she turned out to be a good one. My raptures with Geoffrey didn't last much longer than the honeymoon. Living with him was like living with a tailor's dummy, not a man. He was always in the right place at the right time, always said and did the right things – all you had to do was wind him up and he went. I'm obstinate. I hate to give up on an idea or admit I've made a mistake, so I usually hang in there as long as I can take the pounding. Not that he was capable of doing any pounding, but I was – my head against the wall. Probably I could have given up sooner if it hadn't been for the baby. The little girl who never was. Stillborn. She would have been twenty last month. A few minutes after they finished telling me I couldn't have another, Geoffrey walked in looking like a magazine illustration of sorrowful solicitude, carrying a bouquet of roses in his two precious hands and – Well, I wasn't strong enough to throw anything that time. The marriage was pretty well finished after that, but it dragged on for a couple of years longer, mainly because he used to take off on long jaunts to remote parts of the world. He fancied himself an explorer, in an amateurish sort of way. Then one day he took off permanently – with half a million dollars. Maybe there was a cuddly little dressmaker's dummy in the picture. The official party line is that he went off on a round-the-

world solo flight and didn't come back. It couldn't be made any more definite than that in case he chose to return from the dead to haunt me. Ancient history now. Now I wonder why I ever bothered to hush it up. Vanity, I suppose. How much more easily could I have been rid of him? The money never bothered me – I always felt he was entitled to it. Reparations. Living with me couldn't have been any picnic for him, especially after I lost the baby. Poor Geoffrey. I doubt if there was anybody in the world who missed him, except possibly the museum directors he bombarded with artifacts from his travels. The whole business seems remote, hardly worth a quarrel with a friend, but for a long time I didn't find it easy to forgive Pauline for being right. Or to forgive myself for caring about things that simply aren't that important. My father cared, too. Not while he was making his millions – he was too busy then – but after he retired and settled back to enjoy gracious living in his old age. He didn't. The treatment he got from the crème de la crème *ate away at his peace of mind. I honestly think it shortened his life . . .*

A living-room, cultivating rusticity. The fireplace is of red bricks straight from the kiln. The bearskin rug is the legacy of a bear who must have taken a daily bath during life. The chairs and the sofa are upholstered in simulated leather and simulated tree bark. On a chair in front of the fireplace, where a good fire is going, Pauline Rourke reclines with her legs thrust straight out, the soles of her boots very close to the blaze. Her eyes are closed, her face is pinched with weariness, and about her is the aura of the archetypal spinster, although she is still on the right side of thirty. A glass of undiluted whisky stands on the arm of the chair.

Another glass, the liquid within much paler, stands on the mantel, held loosely in the left hand of a man who is poking the fire with his right. Slight and wiry and dark, he has a ferret-like face marked by prematurely receding hairline, protruding eyes, and the expression of one who lives close to his nerve ends. His poking is jerky and spasmodic. He is talking. It is clear that he has been talking for some time.

'– just too much. Much too much. I've taken a lot of shit from him, but this was beyond endurance. Maybe it wasn't politic to tell him off –' He stops talking and poking for a moment of reflection, then resumes both. 'Maybe it wasn't politic to tell him off. I'll concede that. After all, I have to work beside him. Literally beside him – the wall between us is as flimsy as cardboard. And he has a real pipeline to Burns. I happen to know his sister-in-law is one of Burns's fillies. And please don't ask me how I happen to know.' A vigorous jab at the fire sends a few sparks flying. One lands on the knee of Pauline's camelhair slacks, but goes out without doing any damage.

'I wasn't going to ask.' Pauline sounds as weary as she looks. 'I'm sure if you say so it's true.'

'Oh, it's true all right, never fear. But my God, Pauline, how can I be expected to put up with remarks like that? He has some nerve, impugning *my* judgment. When I think of some of the lapses *he's* been guilty of I could just – Well –' Another vigorous jab at the fire. More sparks fly.

Pauline's eyes are open now. She waves away threats to her clothing. 'Isn't it possible you're making a bit too much of it? To be truthful, I didn't get the impression he was trying to be offensive. All he said was – '

'I know what he said. And I know his tone was light and casual, as if he meant it for a joke. But the nuances – I wasn't fooled, as *you* apparently were.' Dudgeon is very high indeed. He puts down the poker, straightens up, and faces Pauline, folding his arms across his chest. 'What interests me is why you should have been fooled. You're an intelligent woman, Pauline. You have insights. Reliable insights, as a rule. It's significant that they weren't working over this. Extremely significant. It's worth taking the time and trouble to find out why, I think.'

'Kenneth – '

'Don't withdraw, Pauline.'

'I'm not withdrawing.' And in support of this assertion, Pauline sits up straight, her face all attention. 'I'm simply not in a mood for explanations, that's all. I'm perishing with fatigue. I just want to go to bed.'

'That's all you ever want to do.' Bitterly. 'A man appreciates that, God knows, but there *are* other things. Not for you, apparently. You don't seem to be able to think past the sack. When you don't want to screw, you want to sleep. It's absurd, the amount of sleep you need. It's – '

'Kenneth, please. Not now. Please not now. I can't face it.'

' – pathological,' he continues. 'It's an evasion and you know it. Every time you hit the hay you're retreating from – '

'All right.' Pauline reaches for her glass and takes a deep swallow from it. 'You think I'm an escape artist *par excellence*. You've accused me of it before, and we've thrashed it out before. Undoubtedly you'll accuse me of it again, and we'll thrash it out again. But not now. I really am tired, Kenneth. An outdoor barbecue in the snow isn't my idea of fun. At the moment I'm peeved at the kind of people who think such things up, and it's hard not to feel a little peeved at you for dragging me along. Now let it alone, can't you?'

He hears her out with a scowl, resentment smouldering in his eyes. For a moment he is silent, thinking hard. Then, slowly, his brow clears and a gleam comes into his eyes: he looks like someone harkening to a clarion call.

'Oh, God!' With a soft moan, Pauline empties her glass and slumps down again.

...frequently like that. Much too frequently. It wasn't only that she lacked pizzazz. She wouldn't make any efforts to compensate. In social situations she was impossible – withdrawal was so complete I sometimes felt I had a somnambulist in tow. I never held it against her, naturally. How can you affix blame when it's obvious someone is resorting to her little escape mechanism because she lacks the guts to come to grips with reality? One thing I can say for Pauline, she didn't unload her problems on others. That's not saying very much. It made for peace and quiet, but it wasn't the kind of peace that's beneficial in the long run. It's based on repression, you see. I can't say my association with Pauline had very many benefits, to be honest about it. I believe in being honest about things. It's the only way to live with yourself. Oh, I'm not saying the affair was totally unrewarding. Far from it. Biologically speaking, I had nothing to complain of, except possibly a lack of flesh in strategic places – a man likes to have something to hang on to. But you can't spend all your time in the hay, can you? It's no basis for a real relationship. Yes, the question of marriage did come up. Rather early in the game, as a matter of

fact. We discussed it and came to the conclusion it wouldn't work. In that we showed more wisdom than people generally show in the first wave of an attraction. Eventually the thing simply wore out, as things do. One day I woke up feeling I'd had it with Pauline. How long can you go on trying to communicate with someone who doesn't respond? Knock, knock, knock at the door, and nobody ever home. The break was amicable. Not the slightest resentment on either side. We parted friends, we remained friends. I'd even go so far as to say we made better friends than lovers. I've always felt that when things got rough I could turn to Pauline and be sure of getting a sympathetic hearing. That's a good way to feel about someone . . .

An office. The walls are mainly expanses of recessed book-shelves, and all the shelves are filled. There are two desks, both of oak and dovetailed by hand, not collectors' items but well worth attention as specimens of nineteenth-century American craftsmanship. At a right angle to the one nearer the door is a typing table with an electric Olympia on it; the desk chair is tall and sturdy, with a straight, fan-shaped back and no arms. The other, larger desk, which has the more favourable situation in front of the room's double window (the Venetian blind is lowered and the slats are half-closed against the light, as in a sickroom), has a handsome, comfortable-looking Windsor chair, with additional comfort provided by a green leather seat cushion. The man seated there has a splendid head of thick, shimmering silver hair. Nothing about his face quite measures up, though his features lack neither character nor distinction. His skin is dry, with a faintly ashen tinge, and there are tobacco-coloured pouches beneath his eyes. His attitude – hands gripping the arms of the chair, head propped up against the back of the chair – is that of someone making a great effort not to go down for the count. What threatens to send him down is Pauline Rourke, who leans over the desk, her outspread hands pressed hard against the blotter. In her severely tailored herringbone suit and low-heeled shoes, with the first threads of grey visible in her hair, she looks every inch the spinster resigned to her lot. But there is nothing resigned about her at the moment: she exudes a passion that holds both herself and the man she faces in thrall. The passion is anger.

'You are not Methuselah,' she says in a voice hoarse with strain. 'Fifty-six is not even old. You've got at least a dozen good years ahead of you. At least.'

The silver-haired man sighs softly, but says nothing.

'It's shameful even to think of giving up when you're still in your prime, when there's more law inside your head than in the entire Yale Law Library. Shameful? The word isn't strong enough. It's positively criminal!'

'Please, Pauline. I realize –'

'Don't try to shut me up!' She leans closer to him; her hands are bone white at the knuckles and fingertips. 'The waste! The sheer waste! To think of you vegetating in that tropical playground among people with a mental age of six is more than I can bear!'

'You'll simply have to bear it, my dear.'

'So will you, that's the point. You'll be loathing yourself inside of six months!'

'That's for me to worry about, not you. Save your breath, Pauline. I've made up my mind, and my wife is in full agreement with my decision. It's not a hasty decision, I assure you. I've been thinking about it for quite some time.'

The fight goes out of Pauline, leaving her deflated, drained. Despair enters the vacuum and makes her suddenly middle-aged: she looks as she will look in the moments before her death. She straightens up and walks slowly to her desk, sinks down and covers her face with her hands. 'I'm sorry. I can't begin to tell you how sorry I am.'

'I know.' Relief appears on his face, and at once gives way to compassion. 'I know, my dear. I haven't given you very much warning, but I shan't leave you stranded. There'll be compensation for you. Not commensurate with what you merit, of course. That's beyond price. You've kept me up to the mark the past few years. I would have shut up shop long before this if it hadn't been for you.'

Tears appear between Pauline's fingers. They trickle slowly. 'I'm sorry,' she says again. 'So very, very sorry. I really felt I was building something here.'

He shakes his head sorrowfully. 'The eternal feminine delusion,' he murmurs. Then, with sudden savagery, 'What the devil do you imagine you can build in a graveyard?'

. . . shattering for her, of course. Being my secretary was more than just a job to her, it was almost a vocation. But of course she was more than just a secretary. That statement is a cliché, but about Pauline it happens to be true. Not in the usual sense of keeping an employer supplied with razor blades or satisfying his amorous yearnings or both – my household functions efficiently down to the last razor blade and an office has never been my

idea of a setting for passion. What made Pauline indispensable to me was the fact that she had a fine mind, capable of assimilating a wealth of detail. I tend to think in sweeping terms, and when my interest in something wanes, as alas it frequently does, the minutiae tend to slide away from me. From this you might deduce that I'm lazy, and of course you would be correct. Very likely because I've never had to fight for anything in my life, I take the line that when all about me are losing their heads, why the devil should I keep mine? Pauline, of course, took the opposite line. I'm oversimplifying, of course. I had a reasonably strong sense of dedication to my work at one time. I was even rather good at it. Pauline came along when it had all started to bog down in déjà vu, *and for a while, I must admit, I felt like a young man again. Illusion, of course. The onset of old age brings a desire for tranquillity, and one cheerfully resigns hard work to the young. Contrary to Pauline's predictions, life as a vegetable has not awakened a dormant Puritan ethic in me. I enjoy it. I enjoy being far away from people who hoist the 'Excelsior' banner at the slightest provocation. As to that, it occurred to me, when I learned of Pauline's death, that perhaps she tried to instil some of that crusading spirit into someone who resented it, but of course I couldn't entertain the idea seriously. Not Pauline. She knew when to stop. Whatever she might have lacked as a person, it wasn't common sense . . .*

A restaurant. Brightly lit. Crowded. Noisy. Trays with sandwiches and salads and cocktails in all colours of the spectrum are carried to and fro by waitresses in starched yellow uniforms. Patrons are segregated according to sex and station: here a table of middle-aged men (bankers?

attorneys? stockbrokers?), waving their cigars and Egyptian cigarettes expansively, there a table of youth (clerks? junior accountants? trainees?), waving their Winstons and Pall Malls a shade too casually; here a table of ageing 'girls' who exude responsibility at every pore, there a table of young girls who are gigglingly free of all responsibility. At a large, crowded table near a window sits Pauline Rourke, with her glasses pushed up on top of her head and marks across the bridge of her nose where the frames have pinched. She is gazing into her drink, a double whisky, conspicuous among the daiquiries, whisky sours, Tom Collinses, and other mixed drinks on the table, and her face is pensive. Then, upon the outburst of laughter following someone's delivery of a punch line, she looks up with a mechanical smile.

. . . *She just wasn't a good mixer. Always seemed to be off on Cloud Number Nine or somewhere. I don't mean she was snooty or anything like that. What did she have to be snooty about? Being the boss's secretary? Nobody envied her. The college degree? Big deal. Anyway, she never advertised that. She wasn't an intellectual snob. She just wasn't with it, if you know what I mean. A lot of the girls resented it. After all, we're pretty much of an age, come from pretty much the same kind of background, lead pretty much the same kind of lives. Not the most exciting lives in the world, to tell the truth. That's why, when you're yakking it up a little because it's pay day or somebody's birthday, you get a little annoyed with somebody who's making this great do-or-die effort to be sociable. A real party poop* . . .

An art gallery. The exhibition is contemporary. On the walls are paintings of fleecy grey non-representational shapes, like appliqués of lamb's wool, overlaid with thick, bold, black line drawings that also represent nothing but give the impression they would, if only one were to study them long enough. The floor is devoted to sculpture of variegated enamelled metal welded, twisted, nailed together into shapes that once again defy easy identification. Nothing on view induces shock, sparks controversy, or compels the striking of attitudes, and perhaps this is just as well, for those present appear an academic lot, not quite up to championship of causes. Pauline Rourke ambles beside a balding, bespectabled man of monastic aspect. They stop before a synthesis of pink, orange, and red vaguely suggestive of a caterpillar inching along the ground, and the man turns aside to greet another man. The other man does not return the greeting, for his horrified eyes are on Pauline, who is blatantly yawning.

. . . wanted to sink through the floor. She might have exercised a little more self-control, if only out of consideration for me. No sculptor ever misses his own opening, and since I was reviewing the show – Well, you can imagine how embarrassing it was. She trotted out some story about having been up all night, but it didn't do much good. Odd that it should have been Pauline who embarrassed me in that way. The last thing I would have expected of her. I've known her ever since I was a fifth-string critic who covered everything from dog shows to girls' softball and only landed art exhibits when everybody else was hung over or laid out with 'flu. She was so interested in things in those days. One doesn't realize how much people change over the years, does one? . . .

A dining-room. There is a large, oval table, covered with

a damask cloth. At one end is a turkey on a silver tray, and all around are platters of mashed and baked and French fried potatoes, mashed and baked sweet potatoes, half a dozen different vegetables, half a dozen different salads, cranberry sauce, pickles, and every conceivable accompaniment to a holiday dinner. Dennis Rourke is carving the turkey, while at the other end of the table his wife directs the circulation of the platters with an anxious air. Dennis Rourke, Jr, seated on one side between Mr and Mrs John Strazzera, takes the opportunity to thumb his nose at his brother Roger, seated opposite between a grim-faced elderly woman (the surviving maternal grandparent) and Pauline Rourke. Roger returns the salute and glances at Pauline for a reaction. There is none: she is gazing into the middle distance. When Roger jabs her with his elbow, she gives an exaggerated start and overacts the descent to earth from a journey into outer space. Then, as Roger reaches for a dish of mashed sweet potatoes and heaps her plate with more than anyone of normal appetite would desire, she shakes her head to ward off a protest from Mrs Rourke.

. . . obvious to everybody that she found these seasonal family festivities a drag. But naturally she came. Where else did she have to go? . . .

PART TWO

'IT'S LIKE the boy whose parents came over in a cattle boat and spawned in a tenement. All his life, he feels this drive to make it. He does make it. He makes it big. So big that pretty soon he doesn't know what to do with it all. But he doesn't stop, he goes on, even when the drive is no more than a distant memory. All he knows is to want more and more and more. And that's America in a nutshell. The country that started from nothing and became big. Everybody wants, even when there's no reason to want. Everybody wants more and more and more. And to suply this great, gaping want there has to be more and more money in circulation. The economy has to expand. Throughout history, mankind has always managed to stumble on the one surefire method of expanding the economy – war. That's why for us in America today, as for primitive man in his cave or his tent, it's always wartime.'

The young man stopped talking, and his glance circled the massive, rather battered wooden table in search of a reaction. It was an earnest glance, not without kindliness. The young man was an earnest young man – thoroughly respectable, well-tended despite youth's obligatory badge of long hair and beard (both carefully trimmed), and he sat tall and straight in his clean trousers and pullover. There was no doubt that he was an experienced soapbox orator, the experience, presumably, having been gained on a campus somewhere, since the law in New York City takes a dim view of soapboxes. On this occasion, the law was not interfering; was instead hearing the oration out in silence. Meredith and Drake, seated directly opposite the young man, regarded him with no show of emotion, though, conceivably, the way Meredith was gripping a pencil with both hands could be interpreted as a show of emotion. Another pencil was present in the right hand of a middle-aged woman, doing its proper work and taking down the young man's words. Also seated at the table was a young girl, as freshly scrubbed as the young man and similarly dressed, whose worshipful eyes never left his face.

'It's no secret to anybody,' the young man resumed, 'that lots of us don't like finding ourselves holding a bag we don't want to hold. We don't like going off to the battlefield to keep the dollar safe. So we protest, we burn draft cards, we even set ourselves alight with kerosene, and what happens? The whole sick society gives us attention, we get lots of sympathy from well-meaning, ineffectual types, marathon philosophical flapdoodles are organized on our behalf, and nothing changes. So what good does protesting do? Answer that one.' Again the searching glance circled the table.

Silence. Then, 'It's not our job to come up with answers, son,' Drake said, without harshness. 'This isn't a classroom debate. You said you had something to tell us. Get on with it.'

'That's an answer, in case you don't know it. But not the kind you'd have to stand up and be counted on, naturally. Okay. When the usual protests don't work, it's necessary to find something that will, something to bring home to people the fact that as a nation we're all dancing on the edge of a precipice – dancing ourselves to death, as in the Middle Ages. So I thought of this. A place like

Longfields is a flagrant symbol of conspicuous consumption – I doubt if there's a damn thing on sale there that anybody actually needs. I thought if the act of spending could be associated in the public mind with danger, it might make people more aware. Of course the death of one woman is nothing in itself, but if it were followed by other deaths in other places, after a while people would be bound to re-evaluate their actions, think twice about everything they do.'

The young man stopped talking. Once again the searching glance went round, and this time it held an appeal – for assent, for denial, for recognition.

'I think you're wrong,' Meredith said. 'Always supposing you did succeed in touching off a chain of terrorist incidents, the result would be more guns and knives and killer dogs in the possession of ordinary people who wouldn't normally think about such things. Violence doesn't make people think, it makes them get violent back. Who reasons when he's being pounded over the head? But that's beside the point. What concerns us is the murder of Pauline Rourke. If you killed her to get attention, why wait nearly a month before climbing up on the roof top to do your shouting?'

'Because we were sure you would dismiss us as cranks if we came forward right away.'

'Likely enough. The pig mentality. Okay, I'll buy it. One thing puzzles me, though.' Meredith's eyes, dark and hard and inscrutable, moved from the young man to the girl. 'Why did you single out a plainly dressed woman when the place must have been crawling with mink stoles and the kind of jewellery that goes with them? The only way I can figure it is that maybe you were too keyed up to do much observing and you made a beeline for Pauline Rourke because of the red sweater she had on.'

The briefest of hesitations, and the girl nodded. 'That's right. That's exactly the way it happened. When it came to actually doing it, I guess I sort of panicked a little. Everything seemed to become a great big blur – you know how it is when you panic. Anyway, what difference did it make who she was, when the important thing was to get the message across?'

'I wouldn't know. It's your message, not mine.' Meredith lit a cigarette and proffered the pack to the young man and the girl. They declined, the girl with a sniff of disapproval. 'I'll level with you, kids. We're cops. We have our job to do, and that's bringing criminals to justice. The newspapers might give your motives some consideration if they have nothing hotter to peddle right now, but we won't and the DA's office won't. As far as we're concerned, you're just ordinary, run-of-the-mill criminals. Or rather – ' his thumb jerked at the girl – 'she is.'

'Wait a minute.' A frown clouded the young man's brow. 'I don't follow your reasoning on that. I've made it perfectly clear that the responsibility is mine. I did all the planning. Cynthia was just the agent.'

'That's not the way we look at it around here. She committed the crime, so she's the one who gets the book thrown at her. We like things simple – the shortest and most direct route to a conviction. The Svengali-Trilby stuff is just so much clutter. Besides, you don't make a very convincing Svengali. Beard or no beard, you look like the kid next door, and that's the way every member of a jury is going to see you. So – ' Meredith shrugged.

'That's not fair! You can't – '

'I don't mind, Bobby,' Cynthia said. Her face was radiant; her eyes were glistening. 'If that's the way it has to be, that's the way it has to be. Let them throw the book at me.'

Bobby's frown was intense now. He was thinking hard.

'Of course if you'd like to retract your statement – '

'Never!' Cynthia said. 'If you think you can – '

'Take it easy, Cyn,' Bobby said gently. 'We've had it, I'm afraid. It's obvious they don't believe us.'

'But – ' Cynthia looked suddenly stricken. 'Oh, Bobby! Oh, Bobby, I'll bet I know what it was. That bit about the red sweater – It was a trap and I fell into it like a dumb jerk. Oh, Bobby, I'm so sorry.'

'Never mind, Cyn.' A wan smile. 'You did fine. Just fine.'

Meredith got up, strode to the door, flung it open. 'Out, the pair of you. I should send you over to Bellevue, but I'll waive that. It would only be conspicuous consumption of the time of people who have more important – '

'Stop it! *Stop it*!' Cynthia pounded a fist on the table. 'Stop being so smug and self-righteous! You sound just like my mother!'

Bobby got to his feet. 'Come on, Cyn.'

Cynthia did not budge. She folded her arms across her chest and glared at Meredith, challenging him to bring on the wild horses.

'Now, look! If you don't make tracks pronto, I will send you over to Bellevue. You wouldn't like that. It would be a hell of a lot more unpleasant than going home to your mother.'

'Oh no, it wouldn't! That shows all *you* know.' But,

as Bobby took her hand, Cynthia allowed herself to be led from the room.

The stenographer ripped pages from her notebook, handed them to Meredith, and went out.

'It sounded convincing,' Drake said, and added, with a sigh, 'for about twenty seconds.'

'The children's crusade,' Meredith said, as they, too, left the room with the big wooden table.

In the wire tray on Meredith's desk was a piece of paper. He snatched it up and scanned it rapidly, then, with a grimace, flung it on top of a not very tidy pile of papers. 'Statement from her eighth grade teacher, now retired and raising chickens near Schenectady. She remembers Pauline Rourke as a good, hard-working student, very well-behaved. Well, at least she remembers Pauline Rourke. That's more than most of them do.' He sat down, fixing his eyes on the faintly dingy white wall opposite. 'Blanks. Nothing but blanks. If she'd wrapped herself in a cocoon of cotton wool she couldn't have done a better job of sparing anybody and everybody she came in contact with any hard knocks. By now we've found out pretty nearly everything there is to find out about anybody's life. About the only thing we don't know is exactly how she came into the world, and that's only because the doctor who delivered her is dead. Everything that happened to her afterwards, somebody or other remembers. No stretches of time are unaccounted for. Her past is an open book, and nothing in it spells murder.'

'It does seem as if we've had a look at all the pages,' Drake agreed. 'But you never know, the fluke thing might still surface. It's not impossible she could have had a flash that everything had passed her by and suddenly started reaching out with both hands. People do sometimes go funny all of a sudden. Especially women hitting the change of life.'

'Not impossible, no. Just highly unlikely. Any reaching out would have been more or less compulsive, and compulsive behaviour draws attention. If it had been sex she suddenly got hungry for, the men she knew would have noticed a difference in her, and none of them did. Power? Somebody would have told us she seemed bossier than usual recently. Money? She was consistent right to the end – no spurts of lavish spending or drastic penny-pinching. As for any underground activity, where would she have found the time, working for a man like Adrian Lefebvre? If she'd suddenly started begging off the after-hours tasks he threw at her or just plain wasn't available when he wanted her, you can bet he would have let out a squawk loud enough to raise the roof of the Astrodome.'

Meredith got up and went to the window, against which rain was beating steadily, and looked out at the traffic, scowling. 'Christ, that rain is never going to let up. On and on and on. Dreary. Constant. Going on so long you can hardly remember when it wasn't raining.' He drew deeply on his cigarette, exhaling smoke in a slow stream. 'I'm almost ready to swallow the wrong number hypothesis. Who'd want to kill a woman who wasn't there? Little by little she was withdrawing from everything and everybody, and at the end her life style was as close to solipsism as it's possible to get without going to live in a cave.'

A gust of wind drove rain against the window with the force of a fist flinging gravel.

'The woman nobody hated,' Meredith resumed. 'The woman nobody loved. The woman nobody felt anything much about, one way or the other. What an epitaph.' He turned from the window.

The water was blue, very blue and very clear and very still, like water seen often in travel posters and seldom anywhere else. The plane cut the air above smoothly, descending lower and lower and lower until silver almost touched blue. Then there was the island. Touching down without a jolt on a flat strip of land that cut through verdure from the water's edge to a circular clearing with a hangar, the plane taxied up to the hangar and stopped. Two men emerged from the passenger compartment. The first, big and muscular, dressed in a beige lightweight worsted suit and a brown-on-white silk print sport shirt, had an indoors man's pallor emphasized by sleek, dark hair and sinister-looking smoked glasses; he was very much a presence, as a movie mogul or a Mafia chief is a presence. The other, tall and rangy and sandy-haired, wearing rumpled tweeds, had the look of one at home in laboratory or library. They walked quickly to a black Mercedes sedan parked at the edge of the clearing and got into the back seat. The car immediately drove off.

The road went through a stretch of dense, wild foliage, then through a little village of steel and glass and concrete one- and two-storey buildings, then through a more extensive stretch of foliage, and came to an end in front of a low white frame bungalow with a veranda. The two men got out of the car and walked to the bungalow, up three steps to the veranda, and on through an open door.

The immense room within had white walls, white ceiling, white matting on the floor, white drapes, a white sandstone table encircled by three white wicker chairs in the centre of the room, and a single white-clad inhabitant seated in one of the chairs. Colour was visible only at the French doors, which stood open upon pale sand, sea, and sky.

The single inhabitant was Ivy Eastbrook, every inch the tropical overlord in silk shirt and sharkskin trousers. 'Which one of you Bobbsey Twins is Nikkelson?' Her raucous voice made no attempt at civility; her deep-set dark eyes, ringed with testimony to sleeplessness, held no welcome.

'I am,' the man in the sunglasses said, with an impudent grin.

'Meredith said you were the best. No one would think it to look at you.'

'That's why I'm the best. Sandy here is next best.'

The corners of Ivy's mouth twitched briefly. She motioned her visitors to chairs, reached for the bottle of whisky on the table, and poured drinks – generous drinks.

'We had a nice flight,' Nikkelson said, 'in case you're thinking of asking.'

'It never crossed my mind. You've been briefed, I suppose.'

'We've been briefed. From what Mike says, I don't think we're going to be much help to you. We're good, but not good enough to pull a rabbit out of an empty hat. But it's your money.'

'It is. I'm unlikely to feel any pinch, as you know.' Ivy's lean fingers took a tight grip on her glass, carried it to her lips, and set it down on the table half depleted. 'I don't care how much it costs. I don't care how long it takes. I don't care if I have to subsidize your organizations for the next ten years. What can you do that the police can't?'

'Spadework. They've done plenty, but they have to

stop somewhere. We don't. We can dig deep into the background of everybody who was ever close to her and find out everything there is to know about them. We can smoke out everybody she ever said "Excuse me" to on the subway and ask a lot of questions and get a lot of information that's of no damn use to anybody under the sun. We can – '

'It doesn't sound very promising.'

'Nobody's holding out any hopes, Miss Eastbrook. Mike says the one real possibility is that it's something connected with her job, some long-range consequence of legal business she was involved in. That Lefebvre character refused to open his files for examination, and you can't get a court order just to go hunting, so Mike's hands were tied. Ours won't be. We don't have to be so ethical. We try asking Lefebvre for a peep, we try making noises of surprise and curiosity about what's he's trying to hide when he refuses, and then, if he's strictly on the up-and-up and really has nothing to hide, which is probably the case, we try a file clerk whose idea of seventh heaven is a mink stole or a diamond bracelet. If there's anything to find out, we'll find it out. But there probably isn't.'

'Because Mike says so, no doubt. Does he tell you what to eat for breakfast?'

'I might listen if he did.' Nikkelson grinned. 'He's a good cop, Miss Eastbrook. They don't come any better. He hasn't overlooked anything. She wasn't working for a shyster, so the possibility that it's anything to do with her work is strictly a long shot. I'm laying it on the line because I wouldn't want you to cherish any illusory hopes. I have a large organization and so has Sandy, but we can't work miracles. That rabbit has to be in the hat to begin with.'

'It's been a long time since I've cherished any hopes, illusory or otherwise.' Ivy picked up her glass, drained it, and set it down again. Her inimical gaze moved from Nikkelson to the man in tweeds. 'Do you talk or was your tongue amputated at birth?'

'I talk. But mostly I listen.'

'That must make you a wonderful bedfellow. I suppose when you listen all the little wheels churn like mad and grind out one inspiration after another. How about right now? Is this scintillating conversation setting you off on a new train of ideas? Can you see a way to succeed where everybody else prognosticates failure? Anything like that?'

'No.'

'I didn't think so. Well, at least I can assume there won't be any manufactured rabbits. That's something, I suppose. All the letters I've ever had from her are in the car. Nothing in them, as I'm sure Mike will have told you. She was the world's dullest correspondent. But you'll want to see for yourselves. Finish your drinks and get the hell out of here. Don't send me reports unless you have something to report. Reading is hard on the eyes.'

Ivy got up, stalked to the French doors and through them, moving towards the water like a grenadier on parade.

'The Press hasn't maligned her,' Nikkelson said. 'She's a weirdo all right. They say she won't have servants around. I wonder what she does about meals. Maybe somebody leaves them on the veranda and collects the dirty dishes when she's finished.'

'If she eats.'

'That's a point.' Nikkelson picked up his drink. 'Might as well take advantage of the hospitality of the house, such as it is. If I'd known I'd be flying to the end of nowhere just to be given the once over, I don't know whether I'd have been so ready to drop everything.'

'She's paying for it.'

'There are some things I don't put up with even for money. But I guess to her everybody in the world is an underling.'

Ivy had now reached the water's edge. Swiftly and dexterously, with no manifestation of self-consciousness about being watched, she removed her clothes. From a distance, her body looked as spare and firm as a girl's, the hips narrow, the breasts high and conical. She waded into the water up to her thighs, then struck out for the horizon in a vigorous crawl and disappeared.

'She's in good shape,' Nikkelson remarked. 'But I'm not getting a single idea about it.'

'Coming from an idea man like you, that's a verdict and a half.'

To watch the merry-go-round whirl was dizzying, to listen to the laughter and shouting of the children who crammed it to capacity deafening, but the adults grouped around the contraption, far from feeling any pain, were evidently taking a vicarious share in the enjoyment of the riders. The one exception was Dennis Rourke, who stood beside his wife with his hawklike profile bent in contemplation of his shoe tops. The stoppage of the merry-go-round and the rush of the children coming off did not disturb his reverie, though he was jostled several times. Nor did he react to the arrival of his own sons, out of breath, with faces almost as red as their hair.

'That was great,' Denny Rourke said. 'They've souped it up since the last time we were here. I was afraid Roger would lose his cookies.'

Roger administered an expert elbow jab to his older brother's rib cage.

'Ouch!' Denny staggered and pretended to keel over, shoving a little girl whose face was buried in pink cotton candy.

The little girl began to cry lustily. Her parents began to splutter with indignation. Mrs Rourke offered an apologetic smile, reinforced it with verbal regrets. Denny offered his regrets. The parents of the victim, who was still crying, led her away to less dangerous ground. Dennis Rourke continued to contemplate his shoe tops.

'Would you like another ride?' Mrs Rourke asked.

'Not me,' Denny said. 'I've had my fill of the kid stuff. I'd like to go on the roller coaster. But if Half-Pint wants another ride, I'll keep him company.'

Roger hesitated, then shook his head. 'No, thanks. I guess I'm a little old for it, too,' he said judiciously. His face grew pensive. 'Gee, wouldn't it be nice if Aunt Pauline could have been here with us?'

Dennis Rourke jerked his head up. 'God damn your Aunt Pauline,' he said, with quiet savagery. 'It would have been better for everybody if she'd never been born.'

A shocked silence.

'Dennis,' Mrs Rourke murmured reproachfully.

'I'm sorry, Roger.' Dennis Rourke put up a hand to shade his eyes, partially concealing the pain etched on his face. 'Forget I said that. You know I didn't mean it.' He took his hand down and made an attempt at a smile. 'You know, I'm suddenly starting to feel gigantic hunger pangs. I think I'd fancy a king-sized carton of popcorn with a Coke to wash it down, and then maybe a hot dog so the Coke doesn't slosh around too much. How does that sound to you, kids?'

'Wonderful,' Mrs Rourke said, flashing the boys a bright smile.

Denny met it sombrely. Roger scowled.

'Let's get the show on the road,' Dennis Rourke said, his hands falling lightly on the shoulders of his sons.

Roger jerked away and, as the others moved off, brought up the rear of the family procession, walking slowly and dragging his feet.

'Don't you think you might be letting yourself in for a good deal of unnecessary harassment, Adrian?'

Adrian Lefebvre, formally dressed and seated at the escritoire in the stately drawing-room, did not reply. He was writing, and the scratching of his pen was audible. The shaded illumination from the crystal chandelier overhead left something to be desired, but this did not appear to bother him. Or Elizabeth Sayres, who, regal in blue velvet, was enthroned at a table, playing solitaire. Or Mrs Lefebvre, who sat in an arm-chair with a book spread open over the brown chiffon folds of her dress.

But Mrs Lefebvre was not reading; she was looking at her husband. 'Adrian,' she said, in a tone that commanded attention.

The pen stopped scratching. Lefebvre looked at his wife with a frown.

'Can't you see your way clear to giving them what they want? After all – '

'That's for me to decide, Millicent.'

'But if they've promised absolute discretion, what harm can it do? They're not interested in your affairs. Surely – '

'Please, Millicent.' Snappish. 'You're a child in these matters. How can I rely on their assurances? Communications between an attorney and his clients are confidential. I will not allow interlopers to barge into my files on the strength of someone's whim. I said no to the police, and they have not pressed the point. There is nothing in my files that is at all relevant to the death of Pauline Rourke. It's sheer absurdity for anyone to imagine there might be.'

'But Adrian – '

The protest was cut off as Wallace Sayres entered the room. Though his deep tan and afternoon suit suggested an invasion from another world, his broad smile held full expectation of welcome. He received it in answering smiles, Mrs Lefebvre's somewhat half-hearted.

'The commuter returns,' Lefebvre said jovially.

'It was a near thing,' Sayres said. 'I almost missed the plane.' He shook his father-in-law's hand, went to plant a dutiful kiss on his mother-in-law's cheek, then hastened to his wife and stooped to kiss her upturned mouth energetically.

'Darling,' Elizabeth murmured. 'You look as though you've been soaking up sun at the beach the whole time. I don't believe you've been transacting any business at all.'

'You'd find it out soon enough if I hadn't.' Sayres sat down beside his wife and gazed at her tenderly. 'I arranged for a shipment of Quiché ceramics to Italy. I have a hunch they'll catch on in a big way over there.'

'Your hunches usually pan out,' Lefebvre said.

'Always,' Elizabeth said.

'Some of the time,' Sayres said, with a laugh. 'Sylvia delivered, darling. It went off like a charm. A nice strapping boy.'

'Oh, I'm so glad. I was worried about her. She looked

so peaky when I left.'

'Who is Sylvia?' Lefebvre asked.

'My mare,' Elizabeth said. 'Now we'll have a good mount for Junior, too.'

Laughter from everyone except Mrs Lefebvre.

Solicitude sobered Sayres's face. 'How have you been, darling? You haven't tried to do too much?'

'Oh, no. No one will let me do anything. I might as well be a graven image. The great stone mother. It's too ridiculous.'

'It isn't ridiculous at all,' Sayres said firmly.

'Quite right,' Lefebvre agreed. 'We're not taking any chances with my grandson.'

'I doubt if Elizabeth requires quite as much pampering as she gets,' Mrs Lefebvre said, and received surprised stares from the others. 'Giving birth is a perfectly simple, natural process, and the doctor says she's in excellent health. Why make such a fuss over it?'

'Probably Mother thinks I should have the baby without anaesthetic. In a lean-to, like a pioneer woman.' The laugh Elizabeth appended to this was brief and rather brittle. 'Well, she may be right. If Sylvia could manage it, why can't I?'

'I see no reason why you can't,' Mrs Lefebvre said, and this time the stares levelled at her held downright incredulity.

'Really, Millicent,' Lefebvre said. 'I don't know what's come over you this evening. Is it those new pills?'

Mrs Lefebvre shrugged and gave her attention to her book.

'Daddy and Mummy were having a little spat,' Elizabeth said, in response to a look of inquiry from her husband. 'Over that tiresome Pauline Rourke business. Apparently somebody isn't satisfied with the way the police are doing their job and has hired private detectives to help things along. They want to examine Daddy's files, no doubt on the supposition that some steel executive or breakfast cereal magnate didn't like the way Pauline Rourke took notes and chose an extreme method of expressing his displeasure. Daddy said no, of course. It's too absurd.'

'It is not absurd.' Mrs Lefebvre closed her book, Edmund Wilson's *Upstate,* and placed it on the table beside her chair. 'Why not let them examine the files and have done with it, Adrian? They'll see there's nothing there for them and do their snooping elsewhere. Refusing permission will certainly be interpreted as refusing to co-operate, and they'll begin wondering why you're refusing to co-operate. When they begin wondering they begin speculating, and when they begin speculating they arrive at all sorts of wild conclusions. We'll never hear the end of it!'

A stunned silence greeted this outburst.

'My dear Millicent,' Lefebvre said softly, 'are you suggesting that they might think it's I who didn't like the way Miss Rourke took notes?'

'No, of course not. Really, Adrian, sometimes your certainty that you're beyond the reach of the world's aches and pains can be maddening! From what I've heard about private investigators, they are no respecters of persons. Why should they be? Their job is to find the black spots in people's histories, and the slightest speck of grey can show up black, if somebody has a mind to hold it up to a strong enough light.'

'Mother's obviously been reading those magazine exposés,' Elizabeth said. 'You know, hidden cameras in offices to find out who's making off with the paper clips and hidden microphones in people's houses to find out whose wife is a security risk because she talks to her friends too much.'

'Invasion of privacy is not a joke, Elizabeth,' Mrs Lefebvre said. 'Those articles may exaggerate, but they *are* based on reality. Why on earth should we invite a horde of Peeping Toms into our lives when we can so easily avoid it?'

'I don't see that it's a question of "our lives". Even if they do start wondering about Daddy's motives – '

'If they take it into their heads to probe your father's past they're hardly likely to spare the rest of us.'

'Honestly, Mother, anybody listening to you would imagine we have skeletons rattling around every closet in the house.'

'Your mother has a point, darling,' Sayres said. 'Privacy isn't a word that has any meaning for types like these. They stick at nothing.'

'I'm delighted to see somebody taking a reasonable attitude,' Mrs Lefebvre said.

'What is reasonable about any part of this discussion?' Lefebvre asked. 'I've never listened to such a packet of nonsense in my life. What concern is it of ours whether or not they stick at anything? Their business is to find out who killed Pauline Rourke, and they're welcome to go about it any way that suits them as long as they don't poke their noses into my professional affairs. I don't want to hear another word about it.'

'Don't you think you might – ' Sayres began.

'I wouldn't interfere, darling,' Elizabeth said. 'Daddy knows best. In any event, you're not involved. You didn't even know Pauline Rourke.' She yawned, wide, without covering her mouth. 'I'm going to bed. It's late, and all this chatter has made me very, very sleepy. Coming, darling?'

'Of course, darling.' And Sayres rose to offer his arm to his wife.

Adrian Lefebvre agreed that retirement was in order. Mrs Lefebvre elected to stay up and read for a while. But when the others had left her, she ignored her book and sat with her hands clasped in her lap, gazing at them with melancholy eyes.

The tea-set was Spode with an old-fashioned floral design. One of the two bread-and-butter plates had a hairline crack running from the edge to the middle, and whatever had happened to the original sugar bowl had evidently been beyond remedy, for the one on the silver tray was of unadorned white china, modern and mass-produced. The two people seated side by side on the sofa were sipping from their cups with a formality appropriate to tea at the Waldorf. The man, darkly handsome and just on the threshold of middle age, had an air of gentility that was partly negated by a glint of restlessness in his eyes. The woman was Mrs John Strazzera.

Another woman came into the room, dressed for the street in a shapeless navy blue coat and a black cloche hat. 'I'll be going now, Mr Gillingham, if there's nothing else.'

'Nothing, Mrs Parker. Thank you.'

'I hope you and your aunt enjoy your tea. Good afternoon.' The woman went out. A moment later, there was the sound of a door opening and shutting.

Gillingham grinned rakishly. 'Care for another cup of tea, Auntie?'

'Don't, Herbert.' Mrs Strazzera set her cup in the saucer with a slight rattle. 'It's such an ordeal to have to go through this charade. Why does she always overstay her time?'

'She's conscientious. I'm lucky to have somebody like that. It's true she's a little nosy – '

'You can say that again!'

'Well, you have to take the good with the bad. She keeps the place neat. You're a bundle of nerves today, aren't you, Selene? Relax. There's nothing to worry about.'

'Isn't there?' She averted her face, and the movement virtually presented him with her back.

He placed his hands on her shoulders and bowed his head to kiss the back of her neck, crinkled like crêpe beneath the feathery blue-white wisps of her hair. 'So your little secret's in jeopardy. So what? You're hardly the first woman in the world to give in to a craving for adventure, my sweet. It's not the kind of thing anybody's going to think twice about.'

She did not respond to his words. Her body did not respond to his caress.

He drew away without releasing her shoulders, scrutinizing the back of her head with eyes that were cold, calculating, almost hostile. 'I can't understand what you're all worked up about. Unless it isn't just this that's worrying you. Unless there's something bigger. You wouldn't have gone and croaked your own daughter, would you?'

'No, of course not.' No indignation in the denial: only despair. 'They'll dig. They'll dig and dig and dig. There's no limit to the amount of digging they can do.'

'That's likely enough. Ivy Eastbrook's got half the

money circulating in the Western Hemisphere. The thing I can't make out is why she should go to all the trouble just for a friend. Unless they were more than friends. Was your daughter a dike?'

'No, of course not. If you'd known Pauline – ' Mrs Strazzera shuddered. 'She was so upright. I don't know how she ever latched on to somebody like Ivy Eastbrook. I'm not really sure it is Ivy Eastbrook who hired the detectives. I simply can't imagine who else it could be.'

'Did your daughter know about me?'

'I don't know.' It was no louder than a whisper. 'I don't know what she knew and what she didn't know. I only know she despised me.'

He laughed harshly. 'That's rich. Tickles the old funny bone. Cheer up, Selene. She couldn't have despised you as much as you despise yourself.'

'Don't, Herbert.'

His fingers dug deep into the flesh of her shoulders. 'You could stay away till it all blows over.'

She turned to face him and flung her arms around his neck. The lips she pressed to his were passionate, hungry. Then, quickly, they were both up on their feet and out of the room.

The bedroom was large, but not large enough. Not large enough to assimilate the huge bed with the quilted emerald green satin headboard and the magenta velvet spread; the chaise-longue with the riotous *art nouveau* upholstery; the full-length drapes of cornflower blue wild silk; the malachite lamp with the cyclamen pink umbrella shade. If these furnishings had made a theatrical spectacle of Pauline Rourke's bedroom, here, in juxtaposition with outmoded relics of middle-class grandeur – massive mahogany bureau and matching twin night tables, overstuffed maroon plush armchair, mirror with convoluted, gilded frame – they created an effect of almost claustrophobic garishness.

Mrs Strazzera took a couple of steps into the room and hesitated. Her face was disconsolate; there were tears in her large violet eyes.

'Don't just stand there admiring the scenery, Selene.' Gillingham swept past her to the bed. He peeled off the luxuriant covering, folded it with a practised hand, and tossed it on to the chaise-longue. 'You've seen it before.'

'Yes. I've seen it before.' Slowly, lethargically, she went to the armchair and began taking off her clothes, folding each article neatly. Her body was firm and well-conditioned, but the removal of her brassière betrayed her, exposing breasts that were pendulous, flabby, old.

In difficult murder cases, it is sometimes necessary to cast the net far and wide, and the haul must be painstakingly, laboriously sifted through. Most of the time the wanted fish turns up amid an abundance of unwanted flotsam and jetsam. Sometimes it does not, no matter how many times the net is cast, no matter how much pain and labour are expended. Such unproductive cases wind up, sooner rather than later (police departments being as busy as they are) in a pending file, where they may pend to the end of time. Unless, of course, there is a break, which is likely to come unexpectedly, from an unlooked-for quarter, by a kind of serendipity.

The break in the Pauline Rourke case had, at first glance, so little the appearance of a break that it was nearly overlooked. It came walking into the building in which the Homicide offices are located, walking somewhat unsteadily on legs in the process of giving out: a small, frail, black-clad woman, seventy if a day, with a tidy bun of pure white hair on top of her head and thick bifocals worn with an air announcing that beyond the range of a few feet the world was a blur. She came shyly up to the sergeant at the desk in the main hall and murmured to him, in a voice overlaid with the gutturals of middle Europe. To the sergeant, who was Puerto Rican and not very good at coping with gutturals, what she said was unintelligible. He made polite noises and invited her to have a seat. It was lunch-time. The sergeant was waiting for his relief, who was due at any second. The relief could handle it, whatever it was.

Moments passed. The relief did not appear. The sergeant made entries in his daily record. The old lady began to fidget, and her face looked troubled, reflecting second thoughts about having come. Then she rose from her chair and, flashing an apologetic smile at the desk sergeant, proceeded to give in to those second thoughts.

The sergeant felt a stab of compunction. He had offered the letter of courtesy but not the spirit, and the blood of his hidalgo forebears was protesting. It was a question of a lady, after all. An old lady to boot – old enough to be his grandmother. Whatever her problem was – lost cat, vandals making a shambles of a once self-respecting neighbourhood – honour demanded that he listen to her. He vacated the perch of authority, intercepted her before she reached the door, and asked her, very gently, to tell him again what it was all about.

At this she produced the apologetic smile once more, and, touching and disarming, it remained on her face as she told him, very slowly and distinctly, that she had information to give 'about the murder in the toilet'.

The sergeant was taken aback (who could have looked

a less likely source of information about murder, except an infant in diapers?), but the hidalgo blood, once aroused, carries all before it. He returned to his desk, rang Homicide, and passed on the message. Was there somebody around connected with the investigation, he asked, to whom he could pass on the old lady? He was told that Lieutenant Meredith was very much around and very much disposed to welcome a parakeet, if it had anything relevant to say. An edited version of this answer elicited yet another smile from the old lady, and the sergeant, whose relief was just coming into view, insisted on escorting her to Meredith's office himself.

That Meredith, who froze in the act of relegating the wrappings of a solitary lunch to the wastebasket when Mrs Rebecca Rabinowitz was ushered in, thought his parakeet remark had been taken literally was all too apparent from the look on his face (the sergeant had an anecdote to regale his friends with for days), but gallantry was clearly the order of the day. With great punctiliousness, he installed her in a chair; he asked her if she would care for a cup of coffee.

She declined coffee with a shake of her head. 'I have been wanting to come to you since weeks and weeks.' Her English was halting and heavily accented, but the articulation was precise. 'I did not because of this.' A black-gloved hand gestured at her glasses. 'Cataracts. They are almost mature now, and I see less and less well all the time. So I thought you would not listen, and that is why I did not come sooner. Also, my daughter has told me I should not. But I watch the newspapers every day and they have not said you have solved the case. So yesterday I telephoned the *New York Times*, and they told me no, you have not solved the case. So I decided to come, and my daughter said, "Okay, Mamma, go ahead and make a fool of yourself."' She smiled.

It was long-winded, but Meredith, like the desk sergeant before him, was disarmed by the smile. 'You made the right decision, Mrs Rabinowitz,' he assured her. His hand made a slight motion towards the pack of cigarettes on his desk, and retreated.

Her face turned suddenly disapproving. 'It is a bad habit.'

'I beg your pardon?'

'Smoking. You did not think I could see so far, that is obvious. Actually, I cannot. Everything is blurred. But I have seen the cigarettes when I sat down, and I have seen you move, and I have – ' She frowned, groping mentally.

'Sized up the situation,' Meredith supplied. She had his full attention now.

'As you say. My English is so bad.' She smiled again. 'Please smoke if it helps you think better. I do not mind. My daughter and her husband – like chimneys.'

Meredith lit a cigarette and studied her across the desk. He read, under the frailty of her appearance, a toughness of fibre. He read, under the patience and good humour etched on her face, a lifetime of tribulations (Hitler the worst of them, presumably, or perhaps the death of her husband). But the big reading was, of course, that dimness of sight was the only dim thing about her.

'Okay, Mrs Rabinowitz, let's have it. From the beginning. I'll listen.'

She nodded, certain now that he would listen, and told him. She had been in the Longfields ladies' lavatory, waiting for a cubicle, standing almost elbow to elbow with Pauline Rourke when it happened. She had not seen it happen – her sight was too poor for that. Her first inkling of anything to see had been when 'the poor little thing' had started to fall, and an instant later her attention had been caught by the strange behaviour of the woman standing just behind Pauline Rourke. 'She went like this – ' Mrs Rabinowitz's head made a swift semi-circular rotation – 'and then she went away very fast. I thought this was very strange because when there is an accident everybody remains to watch. That is human nature. Later, when I found out that it was murder, I was sure that somebody else would tell you about this woman. But the time passed, and the newspapers did not mention her, and little by little I became not so sure.'

'Nobody else seems to have noticed this woman, Mrs Rabinowitz. Can you give me any kind of a description?'

'I see so badly, as you know. But with this woman, yes, there were things I could see even with my eyes. She was big. Very big.' The black-gloved hands parted in a vague, amorphous motion.

'Fat or tall or both?'

A moment of reflection. 'Both. I am very short, so most people look tall to me, but I can remember that she was taller than the other ladies who were there. And fat. Her face – ' A helpless shrug. 'It was so quick. A blur. But big. Fat.' Mrs Rabinowitz distended her cheeks.

'Puffy,' Meredith supplied.

'As you say. The thing I did not forget is her feet. Very, very big.' Again the black-gloved hands parted, moulding in the air a cylinder about a foot in diameter. 'Very, very hard to walk because all the water has collected and the skin is very painful and special stockings must be worn all the time. I know because my sister, may she rest in peace, has suffered from this disease. On some days she could not walk at all. This woman was not so bad as my sister, but bad enough. She had also these big things here.' Mrs Rabinowitz stretched out a foot, bent over, and tapped her finger against her big toe.

'Bunions,' Meredith supplied. 'Obviously she wasn't a young woman.'

'No. Certainly not young. But not old either. A woman who no longer cares how she looks. She dyes the hair red, that is all. It is not attractive. She was not the kind of woman – ' A hesitation, and then, with firmness, 'She was not the kind of woman I expect to see in Longfields.'

Which meant, Meredith knew, that Mrs Rabinowitz thought the woman low-class – phrasing that grateful refugees who had been given a generous welcome by a society in theory classless could never bring themselves to use. He asked Mrs Rabinowitz what else she remembered.

But Mrs Rabinowitz had exhausted her small store of recollection. She apologized for her failing eyesight and for not having answered the police appeal sooner; she was told 'better late than never' and offered a taxi ride home, courtesy of the New York Police Department (actually courtesy of Lieutenant Meredith, but what she didn't know about the workings of bureaucracy wouldn't hurt her). Almost the moment the door closed behind her, the description she had provided was circulated through the building and sent out to the precincts. 'Not that I expect anything to come of it,' Meredith remarked to Sergeant Drake upon the latter's return from lunch. 'Sounds like a description of a pickpocket who might have got the wind up when she saw the commotion. Somebody cunning enough for a crime like this would probably be cunning enough to stand around innocently for a few minutes before bugging out. Still, you never know. There's always the possibility of panic.'

'A specimen like this babe would have been a pretty unusual sight in a place like Longfields,' Drake objected. 'You'd think some of those other women would have noticed her.'

'You would, wouldn't you? But they're ladies, remember. They've been well brought up. Doing their stuff in the lavatory is a private affair – they wouldn't be staring at their neighbours while they're waiting. Or maybe it's simply a question of the human capacity for shutting out unwelcome sights. If Mrs Rabinowitz says a woman like that was there, she was there. She might not have anything to do with us, but she was there.'

For most of the afternoon it seemed as though Meredith's negative expectations would be met, and then, very late, he received a telephone call from a West Side precinct. 'This is Hy Goldman, Lieutenant. I have a notion this pin-up girl of yours could be Jessie Weems.'

Meredith knew all about Hy Goldman: a detective nearing retirement who had never made rank because of lone wolf tendencies, reputed to have a memory like a file cabinet and a matchless knowledge of what went on in his precinct, which encompassed Hell's Kitchen, one of the toughest districts in Manhattan. But the name of Jessie Weems failed to ring a bell.

'Before your time, son.' A chuckle came over the wire. 'She made her little splash more than twenty years ago. Though I wouldn't exactly describe her as law-abiding since. What's it all about?'

'That hypodermic killing in Longfields.'

'Is that so?' A note of excitement in Goldman's voice. 'Jessie used to be a nurse. She started out right. Have a look in the files. She'll be there.' A pause, and then, with unmistakable eagerness, 'I can drop by your office in a little while to fill you in on a few things that aren't in the files, if you'd like.'

'I'd like it very much.'

Jessie Weems had indeed started out right. She had been a registered nurse and, presumably, a good one, since she had held down a job at the Matrona Centre in Westchester County for more than five years. A plum job, no question about it – the Matrona was the maternity hospital to which everybody who was somebody in the greater New York area went for her lying-in. Too rich a plum for Jessie Weems, evidently, for one of those somebodies had persuaded her to requisition some drugs the attending physician had omitted to prescribe, and all hell had broken loose at the Matrona, probably for the one and only time in its history. Result: a stiff prison term for Jessie Weems and, of course, automatic expulsion from a profession that gave no second chances. After prison, an unsuccessful attempt to make out as a practical nurse, and then the slow, steady, inexorable decline into the life of the small-time female criminal, a life of subsistence on prostitution and petty larceny in the main. But murder?

Meredith examined the three photographs in Jessie Weems's folder. The earliest, dating from the Matrona brouhaha, showed a broad, placid, almost bovine countenance. It couldn't be described as intelligent, but it wasn't stupid either. It looked capable, in spite of the dazed bewilderment in the eyes. It also looked pleasant, like a façade with a fair share of kindness and good nature behind it. Had the good nature been a factor in the smash-up? Had Jessie Weems been unable to resist a patient's sob story? Or had it simply been the money she had been unable to resist? The Second World War had left her a widow with an infant daughter to support. She had risen to the challenge, gone back to the work she had trained for before her marriage and made a success of it, but conceivably the blow that had cast a secure young wife and mother adrift had done irreparable damage to the moral fibre. Or was it that there hadn't been much moral fibre to begin with? Certainly there was no sign of any in photograph number two, taken ten years later. A typical mug shot of the kind of face that passed through police offices with depressing regularity – blowsy, hard-bitten, defiant. No trace of kindness or good nature. In the third photograph, which was only two years old, the face was puffy, with the sodden look that is the usual sign of confirmed alcoholism, and almost dehumanized. A face to disturb the mental tranquillity of Mrs Rebecca Rabinowitz, without a doubt. But murder? There was considerable doubt.

Waiting for Hy Goldman to show up, lighting one cigarette from the stub of the last, Meredith was disinclined to turn any handsprings just yet. Petty criminals did not kill, as a rule, unless it was a question of panic when caught in the act of committing a crime, or of a little too much spleen vented during a brawl. Neither contingency applied to the murder of Pauline Rourke, an elaborate crime, plotted with care and cunning. Unimaginable that the wreck of humanity Jessie Weems had become could have thought up anything so fancy. As for carrying it out, that might be a different story. As an instrument, Jessie Weems was distinctly a possibility. People hired guns to do their dirty work all too frequently. So far, nothing on record about hired hypodermics. But why not? There had to be a first time for everything. Still, no handsprings. Not yet.

Hy Goldman, who was in a much better position to hazard an opinion on Jessie Weems, was as sceptical of her master-minding potential as Meredith. A big, burly man with a thick shock of white hair and a red face and the general appearance of the stage cop ('I'm three-quarters Irish. About all I inherited from my Jewish grandfather was the name'), Goldman quickly made it plain that his reputation in the department was well founded.

'Jessie's a lush. Stinko most of her waking time. If she had a grievance, she'd probably opt for a nice, straight-forward disembowelling with the bread knife. Even going through the sweat of rustling up a gun – and it wouldn't be too much of a sweat in Hell's Kitchen – would be beyond her. She's a lazy old bitch. Also, it's not easy for her to get around. She suffers from œdema. Heart, I think, but it could be kidneys. Or maybe both, the way she goes at the booze. Hardly ever leaves the house these days, except to tank up at the neighbourhood hangouts where they'll let her run up a tab. When she's flush she doesn't even do that – just sends for a supply from the liquor store and goes at it till the well runs dry. The only way I can see Jessie in on a kill like this is for somebody to put a wad in her hand, give her instructions, and promise her another wad when the job's done.'

'That's pretty much the way I figure it, too,' Meredith said. 'I can't say I'm wild about it, though. This isn't a Hell's Kitchen crime. It wouldn't originate with the two-bit maulers and drifters and hustlers and junkies and the rest of the pack she's been running with for years and years. You say she doesn't get around much, so that means anybody who wanted her services would have to seek her out. But how would anybody get on to her? Nothing she's been up to in recent years would rate a mention in the press, even when there's a dearth of sensationalism. According to her record, the only big thing she's ever been involved in is the Matrona business, and that was twenty-one years ago. That's a long time.'

'It made a big stink. Headlines. Breach of trust and all that. You know what these hospital scandals are like. Especially when an outfit like the Matrona is involved. Spotless reputation up to then. They couldn't make enough of a show of washing their hands so everybody could watch them doing it. It's not hard to see why they pressed all the panic buttons. Reputation is reputation. They're careful about who they hire. They're also careful about the patients they admit. Not that they won't take dipsos and addicts if the money is there, but the supervision is strict. The woman who got at Jessie was a dark horse. Nobody knew about her habit – her husband and her personal physician were keeping the skeleton under wraps. When the roof fell in, nobody at the Matrona tried to cover up for her. She didn't get the book thrown at her the way Jessie did, naturally, but she did get shipped off to take a cure. Like I said, a very big stink.'

'And maybe the smell has lingered in somebody's nostrils for a couple of decades,' Meredith said, without enthusiasm. He lit a cigarette and offered one to Goldman, who declined with a headshake and proceeded to take tobacco and cigarette paper out of his pocket and assemble his own. 'Well, we'll take a look at the Matrona for a connection between Pauline Rourke and anybody who was around the place in Jessie Weems's day, but it looks like a very long shot. If Jessie Weems is our girl, it could just as easily be that somebody who wanted a particular job done pulled her out of a newspaper file. And how could he know she'd be willing to do it? There's quite a distance between stealing drugs and killing, and acting on the assumption that she'd travelled the distance would be taking a big gamble. I'm not saying it couldn't have happened that way, but – ' A shrug. 'All we really have is a description that places Jessie Weems or somebody who looks like her on the scene, and the witness is one who'd be laughed out of any court in the – ' Meredith broke off abruptly.

Hy Goldman was licking his cigarette paper with a relish that said the canary had proved an eminently satisfactory meal.

'Okay, let's have it. Whatever it is you're sitting on.'

The cigarette-making apparatus was restored to the pocket; the newly made cigarette was lighted, puffed at with deliberation. Then Goldman grinned, terminating his affectation of nonchalance, and years were suddenly lifted from his broad, ruddy face. 'A little something for you. Before I came over here I thought I'd mosey on over to the liquor store where Jessie gets her supplies, and what do you know? Just around the time it happened, she telephoned to tell them to stock up on Dewar's. That's her brand when she can afford it. She's been having it delivered steady ever since, like you or I might have the milkman deliver the milk. Cash on the line, naturally.' Another deliberate puff at the cigarette, and Goldman leaned back in his chair, his face now bland and innocent. 'That say anything to you?'

'A little something.' Meredith met innocence with innocence. 'You know, I'm just wondering what kind of a life they lead over at your precinct. If I commandeered your services for a couple of days, would anybody over there be likely to start an ulcer?'

'Well, now, I shouldn't think so.' A sparkle appeared in Goldman's eyes. 'They've got a whole flock of bright young lads to handle the really important work. Up to the eyes in the latest methods, the lot of them, and a back number like me tends to get underfoot a little. You might tell them you need me to get your files in shape. They'll think that's just about my speed.'

The eyes appeared scarcely more than slits, deeply embedded in bloated flesh. Then a glimpse of moist blue irises, darting furtively from side to side – the inevitable analogy was with animals in cages – and plainly not liking what they saw.

'Open up, Jessie.' Hy Goldman's foot was wedged into the aperture between the door and the frame, having gone in the instant the door started to open. 'We want to pow-wow.'

Compliance was not forthcoming. The eyes – eyes of the inveterate cop-hater – defied.

'We can get a warrant if we have to. You wouldn't want to put us to all that trouble, would you?'

The bait was scorned. The eyes recognized bluff; recognized that a real threat would have come forearmed with a warrant. But they also recognized the law's power of harassment. For a moment, they calculated. Then the door opened wide, and Jessie Weems blocked the doorway.

Meredith, who was not squeamish, felt his stomach give a brief heave of protest, but then only intestines of cast iron would have failed to react to the double-barrelled assault of alcohol fumes and the initial sight of Jessie Weems. The most recent photograph in her folder, bad as it was, had not been adequate preparation. Not for the mountainous frame in a dirty seersucker dress with sleeves ending high on the flabby arms. Not for the ballooning flesh of the legs in surgical stockings and torn slippers, once beige but now the colour of mud. Not even for the face, an amorphous, doughy mass in which only the eyes looked alive, surrounded by tangles of hair dyed jet black recently, but not recently enough. Everything about her bespoke the neglect of the long-time derelict, as far down in degradation as a human being could go.

'It's not business for the neighbours, Jessie,' Goldman said. 'Better clear the driveway.'

Silently, Jessie Weems stepped out of the way. The slits fixed hard on Meredith's face, and the animal behind the bars flashed alarm and then was still.

Inside the door was the living-room, an almost cubic box with a door opposite leading to another box and beyond another door leading to another box – the typical railroad flat layout. Shabbiness, disorder, and dirt offended the eye, alcohol and a stale, sour smell offended the nose, but there was no mistaking the fact that the room, like its occupant, had started out right. Somebody had once cared enough to select the cream-coloured flowered wallpaper, now stained and flaking; to match the pink of the flowers in the enamel of the woodwork, now so encrusted with filth that the original colour could be glimpsed only in spots; to match the green of stems and leaves in the upholstery of the sofa and twin arm-chairs, now sagging and splitting and spewing up dirty grey stuffing. The furniture, massive pieces of solid mahogany or mahogany veneer, would have been impressive twenty or thirty years back, but now the wood was scratched and dull, except for the cabinet of the large and patently new television set. There was even a carpet – thread-bare, with a Persian motif all but indistinguishable under an accumulation of grime and lint, but definitely a carpet. Not a room to suit everyone's taste, granted, but a room somebody had once taken pride in. Pride had long since been abandoned, along with everything else.

No, not quite everything. Meredith's eye was drawn to the numerous, lavishly gilded religious prints hanging on the walls at eye level: the glass in the frames was free from dust. So, too, were the plaster madonna and child standing on the television set beside a Bible, the only book in the room, and the large gold crucifix on the wall above.

Jessie Weems had closed the door and was standing with her back against it, her arms dangling awkwardly at her sides. The bloated face was impassive, and the slits were meeting Goldman's hard stare, a routine police intimidation technique, with no sign of fear.

Strategy that does not work is quickly abandoned. Goldman grinned at her. 'Better park yourself in a chair, Jessie.' His tone was friendly. 'This'll take a while.'

Jessie did not budge. Intimidation, friendliness – it was all the same to her. She had taken up her stance to wait for the punch, and she was waiting.

'Since when have you been doing your shopping at Longfields, Jessie?'

There it was, right between the eyes, but it provoked not so much as the flicker of an eyelash. A wooden Indian had nothing on Jessie Weems.

Goldman evinced no disappointment. His ruddy face was placid, and his eyes looked at Jessie almost affectionately. He swept a hand over a mahogany side table and hoisted himself up on it. He tilted his hat back from his forehead and took a cigar from his pocket. Slowly, carefully, he peeled off the cellophane, lit the cigar, and puffed at it. Playing the stage cop to the hilt, he gave Jessie a wink.

'Funny place for you to be hanging out.' The tone was friendlier than ever. 'It's over on the East Side, and I asked myself how you happened to wander over there. You're not exactly the typical Longfields fashion plate, are you? So there has to be some other reason. What could it be? I know some people believe in doing their Christmas shopping early, but eight months is pretty ridiculous.'

The bloated face was a mask; the slits were dull and empty.

'Or did you just sashay in off the street to use the toilet? If you did, you sure chose yourself a dramatic moment. A woman died there. Somebody jabbed her with a hypo full of Dexamyl. You wouldn't know anything about that, would you, Jessie? So you could maybe give us an eye-witness report and save us a lot of wear on our big flat feet?'

No response.

'We got a make on you, Jessie.' Goldman's tone was appreciably harder, though still conversational. 'Descriptions that fit you to a T. You're not exactly the type to blend into a crowd, you know. Our witnesses shouldn't have a bit of trouble picking you out of an identity parade, even if you have changed the colour of your hair. Why did you change it? That in itself makes me a little suspicious, Jessie. You've been a redhead for years.'

Again no response. No sign that there would be a response if the questioning went on till doomsday.

'What made you decide to change all of a sudden, Jessie?' A pause, and then, viciously, 'Did somebody finally clue you in that a head like a fire engine made you look like your own grandmother?'

That roused her. Anger flashed in the slits. The fleshy, slack lips parted. 'Fuck you, copper.' The syllables were uninflected and rapid – hailstones striking a window pane.

Goldman rotated his cigar in his mouth. He puffed at it. He took it out of his mouth and gave Jessie another wink. 'That was hitting below the belt, eh, Jessie? The fact is, I didn't mean it. I liked you as a redhead. It suited you. Why the hell did you go and change it?'

But she was not to be drawn again. The animal in the cage was a possum.

'How much did you get, Jessie?' A bull's bellow, with truncheon and rubber hose and the rest of the bogeyman paraphernalia behind it. 'A lot? I hope so, for your sake. You'll need it all. You'll be an old, old woman when you get out. If you get out. It's a permissive age, but we still take murder pretty seriously. Let me introduce my colleague. I bet you've been wondering about him.' Goldman gestured with his cigar. 'Lieutenant Meredith. Homicide.'

The possum came to life, followed the movement of the cigar, subjected Meredith to an intent scrutiny. A flicker of alarm behind the bars, and all went blank again.

'We've got you dead to rights, Jessie. You don't imagine a lieutenant of Homicide wastes his time chasing after every lead, do you? You don't have the chance of a snowball in hell to beat this rap, Jessie. Unless – ' A pause that was sheer melodrama.

No response. There was no theatrical bent in Jessie Weems.

'Unless you decide to co-operate with us,' Goldman

resumed. 'We know you didn't think this one up yourself, Jessie, and we're not anxious to send you up for a long stretch. You're getting on. We don't like putting old ladies behind bars. They have a funny habit of dying there, and it looks bad for us. We don't mind too much. We can take it. But can you? It's been a few years since you were inside, but it's not a thing you forget, is it, Jessie? Dry. Bone dry. Not even a sip of apple cider to wet your whistle, and you need something a lot stronger than cider to wet yours, eh, Jessie?' His voice became soft and coaxing. 'Aw, come on, woman, use your head. Why should you be the one to take the rap? Why not shop the master mind? All you got paid for was doing a job. You can't expect us to believe loyalty is covered by that measly couple of hundred bucks.'

Something sly peeped out between the bars, something that wanted to say, 'If you only knew what I know – ' But something else dropped the cover over the cage. Fast. What that second something said was, 'Fuck you, copper.'

'You're making a big mistake, Jessie,' Goldman said. 'A helluva big mistake.' He sighed heavily and climbed down from his perch on the table. 'Think it over, Jessie. If you're smart, you'll change your mind before we have to go to work on you to make you change it.'

'Fuck you, copper,' Jessie Weems said. And, as she slammed the door of her apartment behind them, she unleashed yet again those three words, which might have been, for all Meredith knew to the contrary, the extent of her vocabulary.

But they had what they had come for. 'Give a two-bit punk a chance to feel he's one up on a cop and he'll show it every time,' Goldman said. 'That goes double for the female of the species, because you're giving her the chance to feel one up not only on a cop but on a man.'

The place they had repaired to in an effort to get rid of a bad taste in the mouth was a bar on the East Side, almost the width of Manhattan Island away from Hell's Kitchen. A hangout for drinkers, not diners, and population was sparse at this late hour; the side of the room whose end booth they had appropriated was all theirs. Meredith, who was not particular about what he drank so long as it was bourbon, had quickly disposed of most of his double. Goldman, who was particular (like Jessie Weems, his brand was Dewar's), was nursing his drink along.

'I figured she wouldn't have touched a deal like this for chicken feed.' Goldman embarked on the preparation of a cigarette. 'The way she reacted when the dumb cop underestimated her earnings proved it. My guess is at least a grand. In cash. Half in advance and half after she did the job, if whoever hired her had any horse sense. A grand would buy anything from somebody like Jessie, but it could have been a helluva lot more than that. The trouble with me is, I've spent so much time around punks I tend to think in terms of punk values. Could be whoever hired her didn't have that limitation. Could be whoever hired her overpaid by plenty, if he wasn't in the know about punks. So you might say the sky's the limit.'

'You might. What are the chances of our visit prompting Jessie to give the sky a shake and make more of the green stuff rain down?'

'Almost nil. Like I told you, she's a lazy bitch. Also, she has some sense of fair play, believe it or not. She would figure she did the job, got paid for it, and that's the end of it. When the money's gone, it's gone. She wouldn't think of asking for more. Anyway, if it's really a lot she might drink herself to death before she reached the end of it. Dollars to doughnuts the whole bundle is stashed away in that apartment. Fat lot of use it is to know that. No judge would grant a search warrant on the strength of what you have, and even if you could get one, finding the money's no good to you unless you know where it came from. If you lean on Jessie you won't get a thing out of her. All she'll do is clam up and go into the zombie routine, just like you saw. The more you lean on her, the tougher she gets. Nothing's going to scare her. What can you do to her that hasn't been done already?' Goldman's hand was slowly rotating his glass on the table. His eyes were fixed on the gently rippling liquid and his face looked morose. 'There's nothing for it. We'll have to ask Grace.'

'Grace?' For an instant Meredith, mentally thrust back into that squalid room with its crucifix and plaster madonna, envisioned an altar with lighted candles.

'Grace Weems. Jessie's daughter. Grace Weevil, since she married Al Weevil.'

'Oh.' Meredith downed what was left of his drink. 'Weems to Weevil. She can't be a woman who's had much out of life.'

'No, not much. Just a little bit recently.' Goldman looked up with a grin, but his eyes were unhappy. 'She's on the straight and narrow now, Grace is, after a bum start. The early years were what you'd expect. Reform school. Graduation to the Women's House of Detention. You know how it is for a jailbird's offspring. Then all of a sudden she latched on to Al Weevil. He was a tenth-rate pug at the time. She pulled him out of the ring before there was too much brain damage. He's a little slow now. Maybe he always was a little slow. Grace would be the one to know. They went to grade school together in Yonkers. Probably he sat behind her and pulled her pigtails – they seat them alphabetically, you know. Anyway, it was sort of a joke to everybody at first, the way she took this big gorilla under her wing. The blind leading the blind. But damned if everybody didn't stop laughing pretty fast. It turned out there's something Al has a real flair for, slow as he is. Cooking.'

'*Cooking*?'

'Yup. The guy's nuts about concocting messes in the kitchen. Damn good at it, too. He and Grace started a restaurant on the strength of it. Not much more than a coffee shop, and probably not up to gourmet standards, but everything tastes just fine. It's the cleanest place in the neighbourhood, which isn't saying much, I guess. They're doing very well. Well enough to be buying themselves a house on Long Island, just like any other solid citizens.' There was a clear note of pride in Goldman's voice. He heaved a sigh and said, without pride, without anything at all, 'Poor Grace. It's going to be rough on her.'

'How hard do you think you'll have to lean on her to get her to co-operate?'

'Not hard. You know the restaurant business. Health inspectors in and out all the time, looking for violations, and they can find enough violations to close any place down, if they look hard enough. Grace knows the drill. She's been learning it most of her life. All we'll probably have to do is ask her.' Goldman heaved another sigh. 'Which makes me feel lousy enough, God knows.'

As heralded, Al's Corner (actually situated on a corner)

was clean, clean for Hell's Kitchen or for a more exacting neighbourhood, and, during the slack between coffee break time and lunch-time, in the process of becoming cleaner – Grace Weevil was mopping the floor. Sunlight streaming through two glass walls combined with the red and white and chromium décor to create an atmosphere of brightness and cheer. The seating (all booths – the presence of chairs or any other furniture not nailed to the floor would have constituted an invitation to trouble) could accommodate sixty people with ease, half again as many with a bit of crowding. At this hour there were only about a dozen patrons, mainly elderly women lingering over that final cup of coffee with the forlorn aspect of those whose struggle against sinking to the level of common bar-fly is doomed to failure. And final it was, for, though wistful glances cast Grace's way indicated that refills would be welcome, none of the patrons had the daring to ask. Her routine, clearly, was a rigid one, not to be disturbed for any reason, not even for the advent of two cops with something on their minds. Hy Goldman she greeted with an indifferent nod – acknowledgment of his right to exist and, in this milieu, the equivalent of an effusion. For Meredith there was a cold, hard stare – recognition of the enemy. The arms wielding the mop did not falter for a second.

In the rear, a rectangular opening in the wall exposed the kitchen. It, too, was clean, and a good, strong smell of chicken stewing with herbs emanated from there (a handwritten note clipped to the menu advertised Chicken à la king as the special of the day). Moving about, fetching and carrying to and fro in preparation for the midday crush, were a pair of Puerto Rican teenagers, possibly brother and sister. At the stove, stirring and blending, sniffing and tasting with a concentration no master chef could have faulted, stood a hulking, hirsute, muscular giant of a man in a sleeveless undershirt, with a white handkerchief knotted at the corners worn in lieu of a chef's hat. As Meredith sat down, this trio disappeared from view, blotted out by the wall of the booth, and the sole member of the staff subject to his scrutiny was Grace Weevil.

She was worth any amount of scrutiny. At first sight, a distinct surprise. She was small, not much over five feet in her spotless white crêpe-soled shoes, and scrawny, with deep hollows above the collarbones visible at the neck of her somewhat baggy white nylon waitress's uniform. Short, springy, red-gold hair and the fair, freckled, typical redhead's complexion gave her the look of the all-American tomboy, the kid next door. But this was no kid, this was the daughter of Jessie Weems, and despite the absence of superficial resemblance, it showed. It showed in the face, destined by nature for a gamine playfulness of expression but frozen rigid instead: the mouth was a taut line between taut jaws; the blue eyes were wide open in an unblinking, untrusting, unyielding stare. A loser, and not kidding herself that she would ever recoup any of the losses. Alienated. Dislocated. Impossible to imagine the likes of her worked into the texture of any social fabric.

The mopping of the floor was energetic and thorough, and when at last it was finished and the mop and pail deposited in the kitchen, Grace Weevil came over to the booth where the two policemen were sitting, carrying herself with the erectness of a drum majorette at the head of a full-scale band. There was no relaxation of that prideful carriage as, without hesitation, she sat down beside Goldman – a choice between evils, but also an admission that Meredith was the one who bore watching. For a long, long moment her eyes probed his face, and then, 'Trouble,' she said, softly and sadly, in a voice unexpectedly deep in timbre for the wisp of a woman she was. 'Big, big trouble. Your kind don't make house calls for the Mickey Mouse stuff. It's bad, isn't it?'

'Yes.'

Grace reached into a pocket of her uniform for a cigarette, ignoring the pack held out to her by Meredith, who got to his first. She struck a match and lit her cigarette with a steady hand. 'What's she done this time? Tried to set fire to the precinct house? Don't bother to sugar-coat the pill. I can stand up to anything.'

Meredith took her at her word. 'Murder.'

'Christ, no!' Bravado collapsed. Grace's skin went dead white against the freckles, then faintly greenish. She leaned her head back and closed her eyes.

Goldman put a hand on her forearm. She permitted it to rest there for a few seconds before shaking it off with a gesture that proclaimed a cop's touch as loathsome as a leper's. Then, with a shudder, she opened her eyes.

'Shoot,' she said peremptorily. 'All of it.'

Meredith told it, not sparing her, not making the slightest attempt to soften the delivery of the crusher – that the police considered her mother capable not only of murder, but of murder in cold blood.

Grace took it without flinching, without flickering an eyelash. When it was over, she did not question. She put her hands flat on the table, the cigarette jutting up between her fingers like a smokestack, and looked at them as though they belonged to somebody else. 'Al and I pay her rent. We pay all her bills. What more can we do? Except keep her in liquor, and that would probably take more than six places like this can rake in.' The hard blue stare came up to meet Meredith's eyes again. 'She's been flashing a wad, huh?'

'Yes.'

'And you want me to find out where it came from. Do your dirty work for you.' The deep voice was flat, dull, dead.

'You're the only one who can, Grace,' Goldman said.

He might just as well not have spoken, for all the notice she appeared to take of him: she had eyes only for Meredith. Then, abruptly, she got up and made her drum majorette's way to the kitchen. Goldman gave Meredith a nod, and they, too, got up.

Outside, Meredith glanced back through the sparkling glass front of Al's Corner. Grace was at work again, vigorously swabbing a table top. Her face, seen in profile, was unreadable.

The television set blared baseball. The New York Mets were playing the Los Angeles Dodgers. The exuberant and enthusiastic fan noises were, as is characteristic of Met fan noises, twice as exuberant and enthusiastic as the traffic warranted – 'We did it before,' they seemed to be saying, 'and we can do it again.' But not tonight, in all likelihood. The Mets were down by plenty, and, as an infield pop-up ended an inning, there were moans and groans of disappointment. But high spirits were quickly restored, even though it was the Dodgers the Mets were losing to. If many New Yorkers have never forgiven the Dodgers for having deserted Brooklyn for Los Angeles almost two decades ago, many have, and possibly the exponents of the 'live-and-let-live' philosophy were out at Shea Stadium in force. Or possibly the brief pause for refreshment between innings was the sweetener: viewers at home were being invited to go out to the refrigerator and pour themselves a glass of beer, while strong, capable, masculine hands illustrated how the pouring should be done, holding the glass slightly atilt to ensure a dignified amount of foam and no more.

Jessie Weems sat in an armchair in front of the television set, her swollen legs in their surgical stockings and filthy slippers resting on a padded footstool. There was a faint smile on her face as she watched the commercial, but she did not accept its invitation. She had no need to. A tumbler more than half full of undiluted whisky stood on the arm of the chair only inches from her finger tips. She continued to smile as the commercial ended and the screen offered a close-up of Willie Davis, swinging a couple of bats in the on deck circle. He tossed one aside and approached the plate. Jessie took a swig from her tumbler and came up smiling.

All of a sudden, pounding on the door submerged the vociferous catcalls that greeted Davis. Jessie's smile vanished. She took another swig from the tumbler. The pounding got louder, the visitor obviously not of a mind to accept a closed door for an answer, but Jessie remained entrenched in her chair, as though the pounding had nothing to do with her. Poker-faced, she watched Davis swing at a curve ball and miss.

The pounding stopped. 'Open up, Ma,' Grace Weevil's deep voice called through the door. The pounding resumed.

A spasm of alarm rippled the stolid mask of Jessie's

face. Slowly, with painful effort, she heaved her great bulk out of the chair and shuffled to the door, to the accompaniment of the steady, remorseless pounding. A split second before she twisted the door knob, she opened her mouth wide in a travesty of a smile.

'Gracie, baby!' The happiness in the exclamation, as in the smile, was a travesty. Jessie stretched out her arms.

Grace pushed them aside roughly and marched into the room. A quick glance round, and she whirled to face her mother, hands on hips. 'What filth! Every time I come it's more and more like a sty. Isn't it bad enough you look like a pig? Must you live like one, too?'

Jessie's reaction to this broadside was to back up against the door, standing stock still with her arms dangling at her sides: a robot. But in the slits above the bloated cheeks her eyes were living, meeting her daughter's without fear. Those two pairs of eyes, alike in their blueness and hardness, were the only visible genetic link between the sodden, brutalized hulk in the slatternly seersucker dress and her offspring, trim and immaculate in crisp white blouse and navy blue trouser suit.

Grace lowered her guns first. She blinked, shutting out an abhorrent vision. 'You've changed your hair.' Stalking over to the television set, she snapped it off.

'Gray-cie!' It was a veritable wail. 'My ball game!'

'Tough titty. You'll watch one tomorrow.'

'I can't. The Mets have an off day and the Yankees are travelling.' The accents of a child protesting against an adult's unreasonable exercise of authority.

'You'll survive.' Grace went over to the sofa and, eyeing it with a grimace, sat down. Taking cigarettes and matches out of her pocket, she lit a cigarette and tossed the pack on the coffee table, like someone prepared to stay for a while. 'Come and sit down, Ma. I want to talk to you.'

Jessie did not move. 'What about?'

'Do like I tell you, Ma. You wouldn't want that precious whisky to evaporate, would you? It's good stuff, not your usual rotgut. I can tell from the smell. Or are you so far in the chips you don't mind a little waste?'

'You know better than that, Gracie.' Jessie went to take possession of the tumbler and brought it over to the sofa, settling down beside her daughter. She took a swallow, smacked her lips. 'This stuff doesn't grow on trees, you know. Not for the likes of me. It was a present.' She chuckled, a sound meant to be merry but coming out hollow. 'What's on your mind, baby?'

'A present from who?'

A split second's hesitation. 'An old admirer.'

'Bullshit! None of the admirers you ever had would be giving you presents. All they knew was take, take, take. You bought it yourself. Where'd you get the money?'

'I told you –'

'Quit lying to me, you old bitch! *Where'd you get the money?*'

'Aw, for cryin' out loud, Gracie! Why won't you believe me? I ran into an old friend, I'm telling you. He had a good day at the track and he could see here was a lady who's a little down on her luck and he did me a good turn, that's all. Not everybody's heartless, you know. Not everybody –'

Crack! All Grace's strength went into the slap. The impact knocked Jessie against the back of the sofa. The tumbler flew out of her hand and fell to the carpet.

For a moment, Jessie was too stunned to move. Her

horrified eyes watched the liquor run out over the carpet. Then her hand went up to her reddening cheek. 'Gracie.' Amazement. Awe. Sorrow. 'You hit your mother. You hit – '

'*Shut up*!' The command yielded nothing to the blow in savagery. 'Next you'll be telling me I'm a lousy daughter because I don't buy you a distillery!'

'Gracie, I never – '

'Shut *up*!' Grace's freckles were vivid against a complexion gone dead white. 'I pay your rent. I pay all your bills. I give you pocket money. What the hell more do you want? A Hilton credit card?'

'Gracie, I'm not complaining. I never complain. You know I never complain.' It came out in a rush, like a speech got up by heart and produced on cue. 'You're a good daughter, Gracie. Nobody ever had a better one. You take care of me. You see to it that I don't have to go begging in the streets in my old age. What more could an old woman like me want?'

'God knows. God only knows. Of all the bitches running around loose, why did I have to draw you for a mother? Why you?' Grace's eyes, hard and pitiless, were on the angry red mark on her mother's cheek. 'Why you, Ma?'

Jessie's mask was in place. Her eyes were dead in their slits. She sat as motionless as a block of stone.

Like a tornado, Grace was out of her seat and out of the room. In a moment, a furious banging and clanging testified to her presence in the kitchen. The din went on. And on. The stone did not move.

Grace came back into the room. 'I found six bottles of Dewar's out there. Plus the one you're drinking from. That's a pretty powerful good turn for any one pocket.

Or are you going to tell me it was seven different guys and seven different races?' Without waiting for a reply, she whirled and was gone again.

Still Jessie did not move. But a change had come over her. As she sat listening to the ceaseless opening and closing of doors and drawers, her stolidity had the character of hopeless resignation – the wait for the hangman. The dead eyes flitted over the room, as though taking their last look, and alighted on the overturned tumbler on the carpet. With considerable effort, she bent over to retrieve it, setting it down on the coffee table. Now everything was set to rights. Now she had only to wait.

It was a long wait. The search was energetic and thorough, to judge from the number and diversity of noises, but at last it was over. Grace reappeared. She planted herself in the doorway with her feet wide apart and her hands behind her back. A schoolgirl's pose, but what school would have laid claim to that frozen, chalky face with the freckles standing out like bruises, to that taut slash of a mouth, to that hard blue stare?

'For the last time, Ma, where'd you get the money?'

'I told you.' Jessie looked down at her lap. 'How many times do I have to tell you?'

'You told me all right.' Grace took a step into the room. 'Why don't you look me in the eye when you tell me lies? What's the matter? Are you afraid of me?'

'I ain't afraid of you.' Jessie raised her head to take her daughter's stare full on. 'I ain't afraid of my own daughter, for Chrissake. And I ain't telling no lies!'

Silence. Mother and daughter stared at each other, obduracy pitched against obduracy. Deadlock. Then Grace came forward – a slow, predatory stalking. She stopped in front of her mother and, with a swift, convulsive motion, took a hand from behind her back and flung it up in the air. A shower of ten-dollar bills descended.

Jessie gave a piteous moan. She reached out to catch the money that fell on her, around her, past her. But her big hands were clumsy, unsteady, unsure: the prize eluded them. She slid to her knees and began to gather the fallen bills from the carpet, and even now those hands betrayed her, refusing to work fast enough. The swollen mask of a face crumpled, and she began to whimper.

'Maybe it's not enough for you, Ma. Here's some more. Happy landing!'

Another shower of bills rained down on Jessie's head. She clutched at them desperately, futilely, and then she gave up. Gave up and collapsed on the carpet in a heap, blubbering without restraint.

'Sit up, Ma,' Grace said. 'Sit up and stop bawling. Sit up. *Sit up, I'm telling you!*'

The sobs were choked back. The vast mound of quivering flesh struggled up to sitting position, became a human being again. Jessie looked round at the litter of bills, and her face seemed to petrify. 'My money,' she muttered. 'You had no right to touch it, Gracie. It's *my* money.'

'Where did it come from?'

Jessie did not answer. Wet blue eyes glinted furtively up at Grace, returned to the sight they were unable to tear themselves away from. 'It's *my* money,' she said again.

'Where did it come from? What did you have to do

to get it, Ma? There's almost ten grand here. *Ten grand*! What did you have to do to get ten grand? Something big, I bet. Something very, very big. Look me in the eye when I talk to you, Ma. Look me in the eye, you dirty, rotten old bitch!'

Jessie did not raise her eyes. 'That's no way to talk to your mother, Gracie,' she said quietly, with dignity.

Grace rocked back on her heels and came down again hard. The movement, the trimness of her shape, the crispness of her attire – all combined to give her the air of a female lion tamer about to go into her act. The only thing lacking was the whip. And then she produced it: a strap of plaited brown leather coiled around her wrist. She uncoiled it slowly. 'Remember this, Ma? I found it in a drawer, under a load of junk.'

Jessie looked up, and the slits strained wide with fear.

'Remember the day I gave it to you? When you came out to summer camp on visitors' day? Remember how you insisted on putting it on right away because your own little Gracie made it with her own two little hands in arts and crafts? You were wearing a blue dress, and it didn't go at all. I wanted to die of shame. I begged you to take it off, but you wouldn't. You were so proud. How long has it been since you could get into it? Years, I bet. It's hard to remember the time when you weren't a tub. But I guess if you hang on to any useless thing long enough it comes in handy again.' Grace waved the belt by the buckle, and the plaited leather dangled innocently, playfully. 'Start talking, Ma. Start talking about where that ten grand came from.'

'Aw, Gracie. Aw, Gracie, cut it out. You wouldn't. You wouldn't hit your – '

Grace raised her arm. The leather seemed to come alive as it lashed Jessie's bare forearm. 'That's just for openers. I can hit a lot harder.'

A red welt appeared on Jessie's arm. She stared at it with wide, uncomprehending eyes. Her lower lip began to quiver.

Crack, crack, crack went the whip. Three more welts appeared on Jessie's arm, the last drawing blood.

Jessie collapsed on the carpet, face down, a mound of flesh shaking with lusty, unrestrained sobbing.

Grace dropped to her knees and bent over the mound. 'You can cry your guts out for all I care. And when you stop crying, we'll start all over again. I'll have it out of you if it takes me all of tonight and half of tomorrow. If I have to flay you alive in the process. Got the message?'

For a moment, the sobs continued as before. Then they abated. Jessie gasped for breath. 'Your own mother,' she murmured heartbrokenly. 'Your own mother. When did I ever raise a hand to you?'

'You did worse. You went on living too long. You should have packed it in long ago.' Grace spoke evenly, without heat. 'There are only two people whose right to go on living I'd stick up for. I'm one. You're not the other. If you think I'm going to let everything I've worked for come down around my ears on account of you, you've got another think coming. You dragged me into the gutter once. I won't let you do it again. I don't give a fucking Goddamn what happens to you any more. I'd string you up on the nearest barber shop pole with my own two hands, if I had to. Now start talking. Start talking, you murdering old bitch.'

Crack! The whip came down upon the distended calves.

With a yowl of agony, Jessie pounded her fists against the carpet.

'She says she doesn't know who he is, she never set eyes on him. She says he called her up one day out of the blue, told her what he wanted done, and asked her if she would do it. She said yeah, sure, thinking it was all probably a gag. But the next day she got a package through the mail – an ordinary parcel, not registered or anything – with the needle and the stuff and a picture of the woman and five grand inside. Later he called her up again and told her exactly what to do. She had to follow this woman around till she had a chance to get at her, and she had to do the job quick, before the week-end. She did it. Then the other five grand came. Same way. That's it.'

Grace Weevil gave the recitation neutrally, and her face was white and rigid. She sat at the end of the bench (as far from Meredith as she could get), hugging her sweatered arms Eskimo fashion against the cold – imaginary cold, for the day could not have been milder. Her hard blue stare was directed at her shoes, studying them intently, searching, perhaps, for inroads the grass had made into their unblemished whiteness.

'A voice on a telephone.' Meredith's tone, too, was devoid of expression. He took a deep draw on his cigarette and let out the smoke slowly, grudgingly. His eyes made a circuit of the terrain and saw only flatness. The nearest living creatures, a nurse and the little boy she was wheeling in a stroller, were some distance away. The bench, set down in a region of Central Park unadorned by trees or shrubbery, was, for all practical purposes, a desert island. 'I don't suppose there was anything special about the voice?'

'She says he sounded like he had class. But anybody who can string two words together without a grunt in between would be class to her. All it probably means is that he didn't have a Brooklyn accent. For whatever – ' Grace stopped, weighing her words. She started to speak again, stopped again. Finally it came. 'For whatever it's worth, she says he didn't tell her the stuff would kill. She says he gave her some kind of cock and bull story about how he wanted to play a practical joke on this woman and the stuff would only knock her out.'

'Do you believe that?'

A shrug of the huddled shoulders. 'I think he might have told her that. But whether or not she believed it – Nobody shells out that kind of dough for a practical joke. Even she isn't that much of a moron. But who the hell knows with her any more? These days she's so – ' Grace veered away from that one. 'This woman who caught it – what was she like?'

'Just a woman.' It was Meredith's turn to weigh his words. 'If it's ever possible to say that someone never did anybody else any harm, you can say it of her.'

'Everybody does harm to somebody.' An incontrovertible truth.

'Maybe so. That's the line we take, too, when it comes to murder. But we haven't been able to find anything. Most people would say Pauline Rourke didn't have much out of life, but she was satisfied with it, apparently. She didn't seem to envy anybody else, and she minded her own business.'

Grace did not say anything. She went on staring at her shoes. Then, irrelevantly, 'You know who I was named after? Gracie Allen. My mother thought there was nobody like her. When I was really little, when we lived in Yonkers, before everything went smash, you couldn't budge Ma from the radio when Burns and Allen were on. I remember how she would go into hysterics the minute the programme started and laugh her head off all the way through. You wouldn't believe it to look at her now, would you? I kept on thinking about that all night. Kept on thinking about what a good-natured slob she was once upon a time, when I was really little. Other kids had the daylights whaled out of them sometimes. You know how it is with kids. Sometimes they make such pests of themselves you have to haul off and smack them. Not her. She couldn't have me around enough and she never raised a hand to me. I thought about that last night. I thought about something else, too. Just before it happened, I told her I wanted a bicycle, and she ran right out and bought me an English racer. Hand brakes and everything. I haven't thought about that bike in years. I smashed it to pieces right afterwards. If I hadn't asked for it – ' The spate of garrulity ended abruptly.

Silence. A very long silence.

'She won't last long in jail,' Grace said at last. 'She's sick. Not that it's any skin off your nose that you'll be shutting up a corpse.'

Meredith did not deny this. 'There's no reason for you to be dragged into it,' he said.

'No reason for me to be dragged into it? Copper, I am in it. I've been up to my neck in it since the day she took her first fall!'

Again Meredith did not deny. He qualified. 'I meant as far as we're concerned. You won't have to worry about any harassment from us.'

'I know. Mr Goldman already told me that.'

The unspoken 'So what?' hovered in the air.

Grace got up. Hugging herself still, she was stooped, diminished – a fairy tale crone who has come into the world old.

Meredith got up, too. And towered. And groped for something useful to say. And failed to find it. 'I'm sorry, Mrs Weevil.'

Grace straightened up, and the look she gave him had a tomahawk behind it. 'Sure you are,' she said. And added, sounding exactly like her mother, 'Fuck you, copper.' And spat at his feet. But the precepts of her rigorous, self-imposed discipline went deep: she took care to clear his shoes with room to spare.

Letter from Chuck Nikkelson to Ivy Eastbrook:

Crystal ball was in good working order, I'm sorry to say. As far as her job was concerned, we can just about rule out the possibility that there was anything connected with it to interest us. We've run to ground a number of acquaintances from the past the police didn't get around to, mainly by combing school yearbooks and backtracking on a European tour she took twelve years ago, but the majority of them asked 'Who's Pauline Rourke?' and the answer didn't prompt any significant feats of memory. A lot of garbage belonging to a lot of people has come out of bins, with a considerable stench and maybe even a few motives for murder, but not for the murder of Pauline Rourke.

Recent developments at Meredith's end prove beyond a doubt that Pauline Rourke was the real target, not just a stand-in. That's about all they do prove, though, and they lead nowhere. There must be an answer, but where the hell do you look for it when you've already looked everywhere?

If you're not ready to call it quits, the only suggestion I can offer is to arrange a get-together for the people who knew her best and have a couple of pros wield the big stick, the hatchet, and whatever else might be necessary to prod memories and dig out discrepancies or even a bit of buried treasure. There shouldn't be much trouble getting co-operation, except from that Lefebvre character, who might balk at attending the Last Judgment unless he got an engraved invitation from the Almighty. The chances of anything surfacing aren't great, I'll admit. What Mike thinks of the idea can't be recorded here because this letter will be typed by my secretary, who comes from a decent family, but he's willing to sit in on the session. I should tell you that I tried the mass questioning ploy once and it worked – I got on to a large-scale extortion racket. I should also tell you that I tried it half a dozen other times and it didn't.

Telegram from Ivy Eastbrook to Chuck Nikkelson:

Your idea sounds like parlour truth game. One step removed Ouija boards.

Telegram from Chuck Nikkelson to Ivy Eastbrook:

It is.

'The effrontery of it is staggering,' Adrian Lefebvre said. 'I hoped I'd heard the last of the wretched affair. Now that I've found a secretary who is reasonably adequate to her task and I'm snowed under with work, trying to put my house in order, the whole thing starts up again because somebody has a notion to round up a posse and go off on a wild goose chase. From the way people carry on about this murder, one would think it a matter to spark an international incident!'

Impassioned as the speech was, it failed to disturb the equanimity of the hearers. Mrs Lefebvre, a long dining-table's distance away from her husband, spooned up *crème brulée* throughout. Wallace Sayres, seated half-way between them, appeared equally preoccupied with his food. The manservant stationed at the sideboard behind Sayres might have been a statue.

Only Elizabeth Sayres showed interest: she had put down her spoon to listen. 'What's the purpose of this gathering, Daddy? Did the letter say?'

'There is no purpose, other than wasting the time of busy people who have far more important things to do. She doesn't even pretend there's a purpose. Oh, she says it's a meeting to pool information, but that's saying precisely nothing. The police have already pooled whatever information there is to pool. One must assume that they have a reasonable degree of competence in such matters. No doubt the woman is under the impression that she need only issue a request, however outlandish, and the entire universe will come to a standstill.'

'What intrigues me is how Ivy Eastbrook enters into it at all,' Elizabeth said. 'She's a complete recluse, if one can believe what one reads. Nobody's supposed to have set eyes on her for years. Nobody even knows what she looks like any more. Like Howard Hughes. Why on earth should she be taking such an interest in a nonentity like Pauline Rourke?'

'I hardly think that's any concern of ours,' Mrs Lefebvre said.

'Quite right,' Lefebvre said. 'She's reputed to be eccentric, and I'm ready to believe it on the strength of her letter. The scheme sounds decidedly crackbrained.'

'Does she plan to be at the meeting herself?' Elizabeth had picked up her spoon, and now it was suspended in mid-air.

'I presume so. It's to take place at her apartment. Whether she plans to be visible I wouldn't venture to guess. She might choose to descend upon the awestruck throng wrapped in a curtain.'

Elizabeth laughed. 'Even Ivy Eastbrook couldn't hope to get away with a performance like that. Why don't we go, Daddy? It might be amusing.'

'Really, Elizabeth,' Mrs Lefebvre said.

'You can't go anywhere, darling,' Sayres said. 'You know that. The doctor said – '

'Oh, bother the doctor! He seems to think all expectant mothers should go into an incubator for the duration. Why can't we go, Daddy?'

'It's next Wednesday, Elizabeth. That's practically on the eve.'

'Oh, bother the baby! I can see myself twiddling my thumbs for days and days, waiting for it to hatch. Not that I've been doing much else for the past couple of months.' With a pout, Elizabeth resumed eating.

'The idea sounds perfectly ridiculous,' Mrs Lefebvre said. 'There's no reason for any of us to go. I do hope you'll decline the madwoman's invitation for all of us, Adrian.'

'Well, of course, Millicent. I had no intention of doing anything else.'

'I'm relieved to hear it.'

'So am I,' Sayres said.

Elizabeth was still pouting. She finished her *crème*

brulée and flung down her spoon. The manservant made haste to remove the soiled relics of her repast, then circled the table to remove other plates and utensils. They went on to a pewter tray, which was carried from the room. In a moment, the tray, or another identical to it, was carried back in, laden with a china coffee-pot. Coffee was poured swiftly and efficiently. The manservant left the room.

Elizabeth had stopped pouting. Her face was thoughtful as she helped herself to sugar: three spoonfuls. 'Daddy, I have the most marvellous idea. Why don't you write to Ivy Eastbrook and suggest holding the meeting here? Then –'

'Darling,' Sayres murmured reproachfully.

'That's completely irresponsible, Elizabeth,' Mrs Lefebvre said. 'Anyone listening to you would imagine it's some sort of game.'

'Well, it sounds like a game. Why not treat it as one?'

'Your mother's right, Elizabeth,' Lefebvre said. 'It's out of the question.'

'I don't see why. Imagine what a lark it would be to force Ivy Eastbrook to make a pilgrimage out of her tent. A unique distinction for us.'

'I have no wish for the honour,' Lefebvre said. 'Besides, she's unlikely to agree.'

'I think she will. It's obvious she's the one who hired the detectives, so she must care. I wonder why.' There was a glint of determination in Elizabeth's eye. 'I'm dying to find out. Please, Daddy. What harm could it do?'

'Don't excite yourself, darling,' Sayres said, a little nervously.

'Out of the question,' Lefebvre said. 'The prospect of throwing my house open to a horde of strangers has absolutely no appeal.'

'Oh, pooh! What on earth is there to worry about? Ivy Eastbrook isn't going to make off with the silver, and the others will be friends or relatives of Pauline Rourke, so you know what they'll be like. Deadly dull and utterly respectable. A flock of sheep without a black one among them.'

'That's quite enough, Elizabeth,' Lefebvre said. 'I don't want to hear another word on the subject.'

Tears started in Elizabeth's eyes. She screwed up her face like a child. Her mouth opened wide.

'Elizabeth, darling.' Instantly, Sayres was out of his chair and around the table, placing protective hands on his wife's shoulders. 'Darling, don't. Please.'

But the tantrum was under way. Elizabeth bawled loudly and lustily, with a formidable display of lung power. She rammed her elbows down on the table and covered her face with her hands. Her coffee cup overturned, spreading a dark stain on the snowy tablecloth.

'Darling, don't! I beg of you. *Please!*'

Elizabeth's shoulders heaved under her husband's hands. Her sobs increased in volume.

'Elizabeth! Stop it at once!' All the weight of Lefebvre's authority went into the command.

It had no effect. Elizabeth continued to bawl, racked by great, convulsive shudders. And then Lefebvre was out of his chair and at her side. He bent to murmur in her ear, reasoning, protesting, pleading, finally promising. The sobs tapered off. Lefebvre straightened up and cast a sheepish glance at his wife, who met it calmly, impassively. The men returned to their seats. Mrs Lefebvre transferred her expressionless gaze to her cup. Peace was restored. The only testimony to upheaval was the overturned cup and the stain on the tablecloth.

A fresh cup of coffee was poured for Elizabeth by her husband. Everyone drank in silence. Then Adrian Lefebvre pleaded work and retreated into his study. Mrs Lefebvre pleaded a headache and retreated upstairs. Sayres and Elizabeth went arm in arm into the drawing-room, where he installed her rather ceremoniously at a table and left her to go to the escritoire, open a drawer, and take out a Scrabble set. He returned to the table and sat down opposite her. Preparations for play were made with a dispatch indicative of much experience. Elizabeth got off to a quick lead and, though at one point Sayres had an opportunity to outdistance her by placing the word 'yak' on the board, he failed to take advantage of it and lost the game. They played three more games with a concentration that precluded speech. Elizabeth won them all. Little by little, her sombreness had evanesced: she now looked as contented as the Abyssinian cat reclining in a chair nearby.

'Darling,' Sayres said, as they were mixing letters for the fifth game, 'I'm afraid I have bad news for you.'

'Not too bad,' I hope,' she said, with an indulgent laugh.

'I have to fly to Guatemala City on Monday. No rest for the weary commuter.'

'Oh, Wallace, no!' The beneficent effects of victory were transitory. 'You promised – '

'I know, darling, but this is an emergency. They've threatened a general strike. I heard about it from Carstairs when I talked to him earlier. I really must be there to look after things. You remember how it was the last time they called one.'

'I remember. No lights and baths in cold water.'

'Not only that. You can't have forgotten all those attempts to break into offices and factories and homes, to say nothing of destruction for the sake of destruction. I really must be there, darling.'

Elizabeth frowned at the letters she was arranging on her rack. They were not good letters: no word could be formed from them. 'It's odd that Susan Everett didn't mention the strike in her last letter. They usually give plenty of warning. Are you absolutely sure there's going to be one?'

'Well, there's always the possibility that it could be averted at the last minute, but – '

'Then I don't see why you have to rush off. Why not wait till you're sure?'

'That would be leaving it too late, darling. I might not be able to get back at all. A strike paralyses transport. You know that.'

'I know. Bother the general strike.' Elizabeth shoved her rack away, sending the letters flying. A couple of them landed on the carpet, and Sayres immediately retrieved them. 'Carstairs can cope. He can cope with anything. Why do you have to be there?'

'Elizabeth, be reasonable.'

'No, I won't be reasonable. You promised, Wallace. You said not even an earthquake or a hurricane would prevent your being with me when the time comes.' Tears started to flow down her cheeks.

'Elizabeth – '

'You promised. It's our baby, Wallace. Perhaps the only one we'll ever have. I'll die if you're not here, I know it. I need you, darling.' Now she was crying in earnest, not with the hysteria of her earlier outburst, but softly, like a waif desolated by an unfeeling universe.

'Darling, don't.' He got out of his chair, went over to kneel at her side. 'Please don't.'

She heeded neither his words nor the gentle touch of his hand on her forearm, continuing to cry with a quiet hopelessness that boded long duration. The murmur of his nonstop pleading was audible above her sobs, but it was sound cast into the void.

'Oh, my God!' Silenced at last, Sayres let his head fall upon her knees.

Elizabeth, still sobbing, began to stroke his grizzled head lovingly.

Violets and bluebells sprinkled the white ground of the chintz curtains and the Formica table top. Real violets stood in a porcelain vase on the window sill. There were no bluebells, but their colour was present in the glassware and earthenware and china displayed on open shelves. The large, sunny kitchen was a pleasant room, clearly marked by the hand of the homemaker who liked her work.

Mrs John Strazzera's pink georgette housecoat, ruffled at throat and wrists, echoed the cheerfulness of the setting, but nothing else about her did. She sat tensely at the table, anguish on her face, and her hand gripped the receiver of the telephone like a claw.

'– damned if I'll have any part of it.' The voice coming from the instrument was strident, strained to the point of breaking. 'If you have any sense you'll steer clear of it, too. There's no doubt in my mind what they're after. I can just see them wheeling in their little carriage load of smut, flinging it all over the place, and sitting back to watch people fall all over themselves to explain the past away. A public strip tease. Nobody will have a shred of cover left by the time it's over.'

'Dennis, dear –'

'It's no good arguing, Mother. If you think they'll have the slightest scruple about parading anything they've found out, you're kidding yourself. They were hired to do a job and you can bet they were paid plenty. They have to show they've earned their money. That's the world we live in. Everybody has his bag and hangs on tight so no one else will take it away. Their job is muck-raking and they don't give a damn where the muck lands. Why should they? What's it to them if people's lives go to smithereens?'

'You're overwrought, Dennis.'

'Am I?' A pause, and then, in a quieter tone, 'I don't know, Mother. I just don't know. Maybe I'm getting the wind up for nothing. But I went through analysis, remember. Part of my training. There are records.'

'Dennis – '

'I know. You don't have to say it. Those records are confidential, blah, blah, blah. But psychiatrists are only people. They have corners in their lives they want to protect, just like everybody else. That makes them vulnerable. They can be leaned on. I've heard stories – ' A pause. 'I've been going out of my mind worrying about something I stopped worrying about years ago. Things happen, but you stop thinking about them after a while. You go on, just like everybody else. You lock up your memories in a compartment of your mind and throw away the key and you go on. They're no worse than anybody else's memories. They can be made to look like the contents of Pandora's box, though. I can just see the muckrakers licking their chops over all our little secrets. Why not? Nothing in Pauline's life explains her death, so it's something in yours or mine or somebody else's. Maybe she threatened exposure. Or maybe she was trying a shakedown. They have to consider all the angles. That's their job.'

'Stop it, darling. Don't let your imagination run away with you. The chances are they haven't gone to such lengths. Or if they have – ' Mrs Strazzera hesitated. 'If they have, we'll all be in the same boat.'

'Some consolation.'

'There's no point in being childish. Try to look at things rationally. You must see that staying away from that meeting is something nobody can afford to do. You must come!'

'Must I? I don't know. I don't know anything any more.'

'Dennis – '

The connection was broken with force. Mrs Strazzera continued to sit with the receiver at her ear, listening to nothing.

The official interrogation of Jessie Weems proved, predictably, fruitless. Other than an occasional ejaculation of her favourite three words, she would not talk, and, to ensure that the police did not exercise undue influence to make her talk, legal counsel provided by the State was on hand. Counsel, a solemn young man with long, lank hair and wire-rimmed Grannie glasses and an air of commitment to the cause of the underdog, was hard put not to let it show that he regarded his particular underdog as a specimen of animal life several cuts below the Yahoo. But he was conscientious in the performance of his function. His alert young eyes were constantly on the lookout for a sign of truncheon, rubber hose, or brass knuckles, sending the message that coercion would be used over his dead body. He held long, earnest conferences with his client, dangling the carrot of a light sentence in return for disclosing who had hired her. Monologues, rather, for Jessie sat through them silent as a stone. Counsel was somewhat baffled.

The police were not. 'Damn good reason for assuming she doesn't know and closing the book on her,' Meredith said. He had returned to the office with Sergeant Drake after the umpteenth go at Jessie Weems and was in the act of arranging papers in a large manila folder. Now, underlining his remark, he closed the folder. 'A voice on the telephone. Just the way her daughter tells it. I'm all the more ready to buy the fact that whoever hired her didn't set up a tête-à-tête because nobody who got a look at her these days would be fool enough to trust her with an undercover mission. He was lucky. She might easily have been too smashed to hit the target at all. Or there might have been a couple of sharp-eyed females in that lavatory to spot her fumbling around and foil the master plan. Any number of things could have gone wrong. The whole business reminds me of the kid who sets out to blow up the Empire State Building with his chemistry set.'

'And succeeds,' Drake said. 'And disappears into the crowd. Who can tell one kid from another?' He sighed. 'I really had hopes of digging up a connection between Pauline Rourke and somebody who was at the Matrona when Jessie Weems was a nurse there. Staff particularly, considering that Rourke's father was a doctor.'

'Mine were never all that high. I've thought all along we might be dealing with a true crimes fan with a talent for research. And how much talent would he really need? Tracing Jessie Weems wouldn't have been hard. Any number of private detectives would have been willing to take on the job without ever setting eyes on their client, if he sent along enough of the green stuff. And he certainly would have done that. Obviously he's not a piker.' Meredith scowled at the closed folder.

'Doesn't seem to be. Well, could be tomorrow's shindig with Nikkelson and Ivy Eastbrook will turn up something.'

'A speck of dust on the Lefebvre family plate, maybe.' Meredith got up from his desk, picked up the folder, crossed the room to the file cabinet. He opened a drawer. His fingers walked over the folders within, separated two. The folder he was holding slid in between them. Slowly. Very slowly. It seemed disinclined to part from his fingers. He closed the drawer, returned to his desk, and lit a cigarette. 'That's that,' he said, unnecessarily.

Drake was eyeing a sealed manila envelope on Meredith's freshly tidied desk. 'What's that? A loose end?'

'The record on Grace Weevil. The DA's office is keeping everything hush-hush, but the shit will hit the fan sooner or later, and when it does some bright news hound is bound to start thinking like mother, like daughter and asking questions. Some of the boys in Records like to co-operate with the Press, so I thought it might be a good idea for Grace's history to get lost for a while.'

'They'll know where to look. You signed for it, didn't you?'

'Yes, but I sent it back. Then I went over to get it again. And forgot to sign. They'll think somebody misfiled it. You know the trouble they have with the alphabet.' Meredith scrawled PRIVATE across the envelope and slipped it into the bottom drawer of his desk. 'Not that it will help her much. What could?'

'Being born again, maybe.' Drake gave his attention

to the pile of reports on his desk.

Meredith blew a cloud of smoke at the wall. He stared at the cloud. When it dissipated, he blew another and stared at that.

Silence. Drake went on working. Meredith went on producing clouds. The gloom in the office intensified, solidified, stretched overhead like a pall. Time passed.

Drake grew visibly restive. He raised his head. 'You were talking a little while ago about catching up on some of the time off that's owing to you, weren't you?'

'There's a nice, subtle hint if ever I heard one.' Meredith met Drake's eye and grinned. 'The trouble is, I can't help feeling there's something I missed.'

'I've never known you to feel any other way when you have to let go.'

'This time it's more than just wondering whether there might have been something I missed. This time I feel I really *did* miss something. Some vital connection I didn't make.'

'If you didn't make it, it wasn't there to make. You went over everything with a fine-tooth comb. Shove off, Mike. Take advantage of the lull while we have one.'

'You're right. Any minute somebody might take it into his head to run up and down Fifth Avenue attacking people with an axe.' Meredith crushed out his cigarette and got up. He went to the door. Slowly. Very slowly.

The afternoon was splendid. Sunny, with a slight breeze. Definitely a day for walking, and Meredith walked. He walked with long, rapid strides, like someone in a tearing hurry to reach a destination. Today he had no particular destination in mind, but habit was habit. The route he traversed bore almost due north and covered a good stretch of Fifth Avenue, where, as it happened, no one was running berserk with an axe. Strollers along the thoroughfare, the majority of them women, as was to be expected on a week-day afternoon, looked eminently respectable and serene: all the hatches were battened down. Meredith's rate of progress drew numerous stares of interest – interest that would not, he was willing to bet, survive past the moment of provocation. Question those women tomorrow, and how many would remember a tall man with flaming red hair who seemed to have a pack of hounds nipping at his heels?

A destination had materialized. Without being conscious of a decision taken, Meredith found himself heading for the Central Park Zoo. Well, why not? No better place to divert the mind from contemplation of the various quirks, frailties, and aberrations the human species was subject to. If the zoo didn't do it, he would follow up with a ball game. Hopefully, the cumulative effect of these back-to-back diversions would relegate the murder of Pauline Rourke to oblivion. Hopefully.

Many people were zoo-bound this afternoon. Mostly kids. A crowd of adults might have been off-putting, but Meredith had no objection to kids, especially when they radiated the exuberance of recent release from the classroom. He ambled peacefully among them, his pace as relaxed as theirs, and gave himself up to the animals. The sea lions provided a particularly engrossing spectacle, the sleek elegance of their movements raising the question of whether being human was all it was cracked up to be. The bears were fine, too, romping with a zeal that inspired some very vocal elation in the kids and a pretty good feeling in somebody who had stopped being a kid so long ago that it was hard to remember what it was like.

All at once Meredith's eye was caught by a grizzly who was off by itself, not romping. Distinctly not romping, but standing stock still in an upright position and looking sullen and disgruntled: the image of Jessie Weems.

He took a closer look. The grizzly was female, so the comparison was apt. One tended to forget, watching these tamed zoo specimens, that grizzlies were killers. As Jessie Weems was a killer. A killer whose moral sense was, by now, on a level with a grizzly's. A pity there were no zoos to restrain the Jessie Weemses of this world before they did harm. Before? There was never any certainty of restraint after. Legally speaking, there was no case against Jessie Weems. What could a prosecuting attorney bring into a courtroom? Not the fact that she possessed money she refused to account for. Not hearsay testimony by her daughter. The only real evidence was an identification by purblind Mrs Rebecca Rabinowitz – and just try that one on a jury. Though there was no question of immediate release for Jessie Weems (people connected with law enforcement disapproved of killers running around loose and she would be held for a while on minor charges), eventually the doors would have to be opened for her. Not that it made much difference, in anything but the principle. According to the police physician, she was unlikely to last more than a year. Probably less, given free enjoyment of her ill-gotten gains. Irony in that. And perhaps a bit of justice.

'Hey, mister, you sure are fascinated by that grizzly, aren't you?'

Meredith looked down at a serious freckled countenance. 'I guess so. But I'm through with her now. She's all yours.'

The boy regarded the bear thoughtfully, swinging his books by the end of the strap that bound them. 'Actually, I don't think I want her.'

'That's very sensible of you.'

'She looks just like my mother-in-law.' From a man standing behind Meredith.

'Oh, Daddy, you know Grandma doesn't *really* look like that.' A little girl's voice, all sweet reasonableness.

'The hell she doesn't.'

A giggle. 'Well, not *all* the time.'

Meredith did not turn round to view the debaters. He was amused to observe that the boy, who might have been expected to be more curious, was hastening away at a trot. Meredith followed at a more leisurely pace. The analogy game, once started, was hard to stop. The gorilla up ahead was Al Weevil. Farther on, the self-important penguin called to mind Adrian Lefebvre. Well, so much for the diversionary possibilities of the zoo. No point in lingering when the object was a holiday from the case until tomorrow. Tomorrow he would be vouchsafed the thrill of seeing Napoleon meet Catherine the Great, who was probably winging her way towards the earth-shaking confrontation right now, if she hadn't touched down already.

A bench in the park was the next stop. Meredith settled himself with the inevitable cigarette and contemplated the empty hours ahead. A ball game would be necessary after all. Cassandra wouldn't mind. There was always entertainment to be derived from the national pastime. Especially when the Mets were playing, as they were tonight. Entertainment in watching them, watching the fans who supported them, and, the best treat of all, watching the inscribed banners the fans exhibited through the stands to cheer the heroes on. Not that he expected to be in on the début of a classic like HIT IT IN THE DARKNESS, HARKNESS or YOU TAKE SCOTCH & SODA, I'LL TAKE RON SWOBODA, but even the ordinary workaday slogan was worth –

It suddenly registered on his consciousness that the immediate vicinity contained a large number of dog fanciers. A disproportionate number, as far as he was concerned. The kind who paraded their much too pampered pets. The kind who annoyed anybody with any sense. Just his luck. He got to his feet.

But a blue-haired woman wearing a blue fox stole dropped to her knees a few feet ahead, blocking his path, and gathered a blue-haired Pekinese into her lap. 'Kitchee-kitchee-kitchee-koo,' she crooned. 'Whose little baby boy are you?'

If she really thought that monstrosity was her baby she was in a pretty bad way. Resigned to waiting it out, Meredith sank down on the bench again.

The Pekinese, it seemed, shared his mistress's delusion. Certainly no real child could have demonstrated more gratification under the caresses and kisses of his mother. He preened; he shook his glossy, long-haired coat; he cocked his head to the side and fixed her with an adoring gaze. On her part, Mamma was equally gratified. She gurgled; she giggled; she screwed up her thickly powdered nose in a funny face. At last the little love-in was over. The happy pair departed. The path was clear.

But Meredith remained on the bench, motionless, looking like someone who has just been sandbagged. Then he was up and off, going at a speed that made his rate of progress earlier seem like slow motion.

Before the plane was entirely at a standstill, two men were stationed near the cockpit, waiting for the pilot to emerge. The pilot was Ivy Eastbrook, attired in black leather from head to toe. She climbed down effortlessly and, passing the two men without a glance, walked towards a black Mercedes sedan parked some distance away, covering a lot of ground with each stride.

A chauffeur in uniform stood beside the car. Ivy waved him away, opened the door to the driver's seat, and got in. She closed the door and reached for a silver flask in a niche below the dashboard. Unscrewing the cap, she drank with the avidity of one just returned from a trek through desert. The flask went back into its niche. Divesting herself of helmet and goggles, she put on dark glasses and started the motor. She drove skilfully, maintaining a fast, steady speed over country roads and a network of turnpikes, slowing down to enter the East River Drive.

On Beekman Place is a tall building of grey stone with a turret – a Manhattan landmark, on the route of coaches filled with sightseers who crane their necks in the hope of getting a glimpse of the resident celebrity. No coach was on hand to garner this reward as Ivy Eastbrook pulled the Mercedes up before the entrance and got out.

'Good afternoon, Miss Eastbrook.' The greeting from an unsmiling doorman seemed to be emulating a recorded announcement, and the recipient marched into the lobby as though no human agency were involved in the opening of the door. Nor in the running of the elevator, though the smile and the greeting from the operator were something more than mechanical. The ascent to the top floor of the building was swift and virtually soundless.

The elevator started down the instant Ivy stepped out of it. She crossed the hall to the door opposite, took a key from the pocket of her leather jacket, and opened the door. A flick of a switch, and an overhead light enclosed in frosted glass illuminated a large foyer with white walls, white ceiling, white carpet, and no furniture whatever.

'Martha.' The summons, while not a shout, was loud enough to carry a considerable distance in the silence.

No response. Ivy crossed the foyer and passed through a doorway into an immense room, where the same white carpeting extended from bare white wall to bare white wall. On two sides of the room were tall windows shrouded with thick, closely woven white drapes, through which the afternoon light came duskily, turning the ubiquitous whiteness to grey. In the centre of the room, four Gainsborough arm-chairs with painted frames and white hide upholstery encircled a round white marble table. The only other article of furniture was a low white chiffonier of painted wood with a marble top. Ivy went up to it and opened a door, took out a bottle of whisky and a tumbler and carried them to the table, sat down on a chair commanding a view of the windows. Removing her glasses and tossing them on the table, she poured herself a drink.

The sound of motor traffic, from which no lair in Manhattan is ever entirely free, was muted and faraway. In the dim light, the barren stillness of the room was eerie, inimical to speech, inimical to laughter, inimical to life. Ivy drank quickly, with even, rhythmical swallows. Dosage, as usual. Dosage pumped into a terminal case. When the tumbler was empty, she filled it again and drank the whisky more slowly. Not much more slowly. Just a little more slowly, in case well-being crept up on her suddenly and she could savour it. But savouring things is for the living, not for terminal cases.

She leaned her head back and contemplated the drapes. They were doing their best to keep the sunlight out. Their best wasn't good enough. It never had been. Sunlight was tough, like the drive to go on living. Tough and mysterious. But if the drapes could not shut out mysteries, they could at least offer a vista of nothingness. Screens would have done as well. Better, probably. That would have been taking the easy way, though, and the easy way was not Ivy Eastbrook's way. Now, with her senses numbed a little (not enough, but when was it ever enough?), she could no longer see the folds of the fabric. Now she saw only a backdrop – a backdrop for ghosts. In the depths of every mind, ghosts lurk. In her mind, they were legion, and each and every one created by her own heroic efforts. A bid for immortality: Ivy Eastbrook, world's champion ghost-maker. Or was that too grandiose a claim? No matter. They were coming now, coming in an endless parade. They passed before her with averted eyes. Like the subjects of King Midas in dread of the golden touch, her ghosts wanted no part of her touch. Why should they? It turned everything to stone. Or ashes. Or shit.

She poured herself another drink, gulped it down, put the empty tumbler on the table, and got up. Going back through the foyer, she crossed a long hall to the bathroom at the far end. It was a very large bathroom, and here, too, everything was white – the windowless walls with built-in cabinets, the carpeted floor, the bathtub, the toilet, the sink.

The taps of the bathtub were powerful: turning them on produced a waterfall. Steam formed quickly, and while Ivy stripped off her clothes and tossed them on the floor, visibility dropped to a few feet. She climbed into the tub and sat with her knees drawn up to her chest and her arms clasped around them until the water had risen well above her waist, then shut off the taps and reclined with her head against the back of the tub. Flinging an arm back like a swimmer beginning the backstroke, she opened a cabinet in the wall behind her, took out a bottle and set it on the rim of the tub, took out a tumbler and set it beside the bottle, shut the cabinet. The arm went underwater. Motionless, she gazed through mist at the blank white wall in front of her – another backdrop for ghosts.

He materialized in the mist like a ghost, the deep tan of his skin tinged with ash, the white threads in his hair merging with the dark in an indeterminate greyness. The look of purpose on his face belonged to the quick, and the revolver in his hand was unmistakably real, but he did not seem any less of a ghost for all that. With no more sound than a ghost would have made, he came up to the tub and seated himself on the rim above Ivy's knees.

She abandoned her scrutiny of the wall to face him. For an instant, blue-veined lids dropped over her dark, shadow-ringed eyes. Then the eyes were wide open again, void of surprise, void of trepidation, void. 'You've changed,' she said, in a voice as empty as her eyes. 'I would hardly have known you.'

'You've changed, too. Not for the better.' Bravado rang out to the gallery.

'For the worse, then. Reassuring to think I had somewhere to go.' Her arms surfaced slowly, as though the water were offering resistance, but the hand that poured was sure and steady. She gulped the whisky down. 'How did you get rid of Martha?'

'A phone call to say you changed your mind and were going to Bedford Hills. It wasn't difficult. Nothing was. There was nobody on duty at the service entrance, and my key still unlocks the door after all these years. You live dangerously, Ivy. Someone in your position is invariably a target.'

'I've been a target since I was born. I've survived.' She set down her empty glass and her hands returned to the depths. 'You're telling me the truth? You haven't harmed Martha?' There was something in her eyes now: anxiety.

'I'm telling you the truth.' Mockery in the echo, and, for the moment, more than the gun put him on top. 'No reason to harm her. She fell for the phone call. Besides, I rather liked the old girl.'

'She's been with me ever since I came out of diapers. Hard to imagine how I'd get along without – ' Ivy broke off and shut her eyes. 'You're a fool, Geoffrey.' Uninflected. Toneless.

He recoiled visibly; his fingers took a firmer grip on the gun. 'Not so much of a fool as you've always thought me. As I thought myself, thanks to you. A fool couldn't have come as far as I've come. I've built a whole new life for myself. It's a good life. Not the life I wanted, but a good life. I'm not about to see it come crashing down on my head the way the old one did. Why couldn't you let well enough alone?'

She did not reply. She did not open her eyes. She lay still, a marble representation of a woman.

'Look at me, Ivy!'

She obeyed. Again her eyes were empty. 'Why Pauline? It should have been me. She never did you any damage.'

'Didn't she? You have a short memory, my dear. I haven't. My recollections of that diligent student of human nature are indelible. She did a lot of observing where I was concerned, and she didn't keep her observations to herself. Remember? You ought to. You told me about them often enough. How many times did you say you wished you'd listened to good old Pauline and sent me about my business? Hundreds. Or was it thousands? I felt I was being brainwashed. As you were brainwashed. If it hadn't been for her – '

'You're kidding yourself, Geoffrey.'

'Am I? How can you say that?' He leaned forward, a plea in his eyes. His face came very close to hers – close enough for lovers' speech. 'We could have made a go of it if the poison hadn't been poured into your ear. You had needs, I had needs. Granted they were special needs, but then we're special people. We didn't start out with any illusions about each other. I never made any secret of the fact that I needed money. I was born into money, I was raised in the belief that the only thing to know about money is how to spend it, and when it all went out of the family I was a lost soul. I might not have been admirable, but I was honest. I could have lied to you. It wouldn't have been difficult, and it wouldn't have been that much of a lie. Money wasn't the only attraction. You had everything else going for you, too. Looks. Brains. Taste. Falling in love with you was as easy as crossing the street. There was no reason why we couldn't have built on what we had. I adored you, Ivy.'

'Oh, my God. Don't say any more. Please don't say any more.'

But the plea was under full sail. 'I adored you. I would have done anything to make you happy. But there was simply no way of pleasing you. Everything I did was either laughed at or scorned. Even the most profound passion can't survive that. I felt I was being eaten alive. Taking the money was criminal, but I didn't look at it that way at the time. I was giving up my name, an existence I could call my own, the right to hold up my head and breathe the air you breathed. A fair exchange. The money gave me a good start. Only a start, of course. When you put down roots in no man's land, you're nothing until you make yourself something. I did it. Not an easy task for someone who didn't know the meaning of work, but I learned. I learned how to cope with grubbiness, with squalor, with crookedness. I learned how to manipulate small minds and take advantage of petty opportunities. It's amazing what you can bring yourself to do, when you have to. I never knew I had it in me.'

Somewhere in the apartment, a telephone began to ring. The sound was distant, muted, irrelevant. None the less, he stopped talking to listen for a moment, then dismissed intrusion with a shrug.

'It took years. Years of struggling, years of playing the role of the jaunty Australian adventurer. I played it well. Perhaps I would have made a good actor. I don't have to act any more. I'm at the top of the tree in my new country. I have a name again. I have an identity again. I have a life again. A life I can lead in this country, too. I've changed so much nobody who knew me before would know me now. Who is there to remember Geoffrey Cheyney? I haven't any relatives. The loss of the family fortune put me outside the pale of Brahmin society, and in New York I was never more than an appendage of Ivy

Eastbrook. Nobody even looks at an appendage.'

'Nobody,' she murmured. She reached for soap and sponge and began soaping her arms. The action was automatic, lethargic. 'Nobody except Pauline Rourke.'

'I had to kill her. She loomed up in my new life like a demon from another world. The one person who posed a threat to me, and her path had to cross mine. I couldn't get round her.'

'So Pauline was really paying my debt.' The soap and the sponge left Ivy's hands and went floating away. 'Nobody ever had to do that before.'

'She paid her own debt. A life for a life.'

They gazed at each other, while the distant telephone continued to ring, persistent yet powerless to cross the frontier they had crossed. He was the destroyer, the taker of life, for the gun in his hand said so. But the look in his eyes said something else – said that he was irresolute, said that he doubted. Doubted what? That Ivy Eastbrook's life was worth the taking?

'Why couldn't you let well enough alone, Ivy?'

She turned away from him and fixed her eyes on the blank white wall in front of her. He no longer existed. She no longer existed. They were both ghosts.

And then he was up from his seat, bending over her with his hands on her shoulders. The metal of the revolver was hard against her flesh, inducing pain right through to the bone. Absurd. Ghosts do not feel pain. And then the metal was gone with a plop, and there were only the hands. Hands that trembled as they exerted pressure. So much pressure. Far more than necessary. She slid down, down, down to the bottom of the deep, and water rushed at her eyes, her ears, her nose, her mouth. The hands stopped trembling. They were sure of victory. They were meeting no resistance. Ghosts do not resist. Ghosts are summoned by others and sent away by others. She was being sent away, and there was nothing she could do about it. Nothing. Nothing at all. And the nothing was taking possession of her, swallowing her whole at the bottom of the universe. Something remained. A light, glinting through a peephole to life. But the light was dimming and the peephole was contracting. Fast. Very fast. In a moment –

Through that peephole came a sudden surge of noise. Pounding. Voices shouting her name, calling her back from the depths, calling her back from the dead. She began to struggle, spurred on by an impetus that had nothing to do with volition. With everything she had left, she began to struggle for her life, pushing against those hands that wanted her dead. As she gathered strength, the hands trembled a little, trembled a lot, yielded. They were no match for her. She could shed them. She did shed them. But the effort was too great. It depleted her. She would not be able to save herself after all. She felt herself sliding back, back into the deep. The comforting deep. The price of this comfort came high, as the price of comfort always did. For this comfort she was paying with her life. Well, fair enough. Never let it be said that Ivy Eastbrook failed to acquit her accounts.

When she opened her eyes, it was to find herself seated on the lid of the toilet, wrapped in her shroud. No, not her shroud. A white terry cloth robe. How had that happened? There was a man sitting on the rim of the tub, watching her. Maybe he knew. Maybe he didn't. He was a stranger, but then who wasn't a stranger? He looked like someone who made a habit of attending wakes – dark, angry eyes and a face that could be bent into a smile only with a crowbar. He wasn't a stranger after all. She had seen him before. That red hair –

'Okay now?' A glass was offered to her.

She took it with both hands. Not a full glass, but adequate for openers. She drank thirstily, held out the empty glass for more.

She got more. 'I'm sorry, Miss Eastbrook. I was a little slow.'

What did that mean? Not that it mattered. She drank again, and memory rushed at her like the water, submerging her once more. She flung the empty glass at the wall. A crash, and fragments of glass scattered over the carpet. Large fragments, some of them. One in particular – a curved triangle, lying on its back with jagged points upraised. Fascinating that it should have landed danger side up. Absolutely fascinating.

Meredith got up and went to collect the fragments, making a heap of them. No more fascination. No more romance. Only a heap of broken glass that bespoke clumsiness. No doubt that was his intention. He must have held plenty of conferences with headshrinkers in his time. The fool. They were all fools.

'You ought to be in bed, Miss Eastbrook. You look practically comatose.' He came up to her, put an arm around her, and hauled her to her feet.

Brute force. They were using a lot of brute force on her today. Well, it was at their own peril. Enough publicity had been given to the effects of contact with Ivy Eastbrook. If they touched her, they invited their own doom. Meredith didn't seem worried. He thought he was tough, obviously. But was anybody that tough? A curse was a curse.

Now they were in the bedroom and she was seated

again, this time on the bed. He stood beside her, looking around at the bare white walls, baffled.

'Where do I find a nightgown?'

'I don't own one.'

He pulled down the bedclothes part way and, hauling her to her feet again, peeled off the terry cloth robe as though he were shucking an ear of corn. In a trice she was in the bed, imprisoned in a cocoon of bedclothes. Now he would go away and wash his hands.

But he didn't. He sat down on the edge of the bed. 'Somebody should be here with you. Who is there?'

'Thinking about that broken glass?' It was meant to be sarcastic; it sounded simple-minded.

'That will be taken away. We like to leave things tidy. But you could always break another glass, if you wanted to.'

Or had the guts. He didn't say it, though he was thinking it. She didn't say it either.

'I'm not leaving you alone, Miss Eastbrook. I'll stay with you myself until the doctor comes, if necessary.'

A threat. Very effective. The logical counterthrust was an obscene suggestion. But probably he wouldn't turn a hair. 'Call Martha. My housekeeper. She's at the house in Bedford Hills. Or so he said.'

Meredith reached for the telephone on the night stand. She gave him the number and shut her eyes, listening to the rapid clicks of the dial, to his voice sending a message to the other end. Martha was there. Martha would start on her way immediately. Ivy let out her breath, and only then realized she had been holding it.

The receiver snapped into the cradle. She opened her eyes. He was looking at her in a way he had no business looking at her. In a way no human being had any business looking at another. She turned her face aside.

'She'll be here soon.'

'In the meantime I have to put up with you.'

'Yes. Unless the doctor gets here first.'

'A tortoise race. Maybe we should place bets.'

He said nothing, and in the subsequent silence her mind sorted out, fitted together. But there was a piece missing.

'How did he happen to come up against Pauline? He didn't explain that.'

'He married again under his new name. Illegally, of course. His wife is Adrian Lefebvre's daughter.'

'Adrian Lefebvre's daughter.' Ivy Eastbrook laughed – a death rattle of a laugh. 'Out of the frying pan into the fire. Poor Geoffrey. A fool to the very end.'

'I should have been on to him a lot sooner,' Meredith said. 'It was all a question of direction, when you come right down to it. If I'd reversed gears and pushed on into the future when digging into the past didn't yield anything, I'd have come smack up against the week-end Pauline Rourke was supposed to spend at Lefebvre's house and maybe taken a good, hard look at that family group, Wallace Sayres included. And later, when we got on to the Matrona business, if I'd pushed forward past the time Jessie Weems was a nurse there, I'd have found out that Ivy Eastbrook Cheyney went to the Matrona for her lying-in a year later, when the scandal was a household word, and maybe taken a good, hard look at that disappearing husband of hers. If, if, if. If wishes were horses, I'd have galloped to the finish line long ago, instead of limping on shanks's mare and almost not getting there in time.'

'Almost doesn't count,' Cassandra Evans said. 'I don't see how you could have got there any faster. Not without second sight. You had no reason to think Sayres wasn't what he seemed. He's a pillar of the establishment in Guatemala. He's Adrian Lefebvre's son-in-law. What better credentials could he carry?'

'Being a solid citizen in Guatemala doesn't mean that much in itself. Latin America is notoriously a haven for people with short histories, and pitching up with a bankroll would have been enough to launch him. The Lefebvre alliance is another story. You'd think they would have checked his pedigree before entering his name in the family Bible. But maybe Lefebvre was so elated at the prospect of having the line carried on he didn't want to look a gift horse in the mouth. Elizabeth wasn't a girl when she took up with Sayres, and her father was probably starting to wonder whether she was on the shelf permanently. She wouldn't be everybody's cup of tea, in spite of her looks and all those tangible assets. Too imperious for a man who likes to feel he's a man. And that's where I goofed. That's where I should have made the connection I didn't make. Ivy Eastbrook told us that Pauline Rourke once described Geoffrey Cheyney as a lap dog, and if ever I set eyes on a man who fitted that description it was Wallace Sayres.'

Meredith crushed out his cigarette in the brass ashtray on the cobbler's bench that functioned as a coffee table. Cassandra, curled up beside him on the oversized moss green sofa with her knees resting against his thigh, leaned in front of him, picked up a sandwich of roast beef on French bread from a plate alongside the ashtray, and put the sandwich in his hand. He took a bite, chewing without enthusiasm. Then he returned the sandwich to the plate and lit another cigarette.

'Those red corpuscles will go on strike. They'll stop in their tracks and – '

'Oh, shut up.'

'Such appreciation of my tender solicitude. It's almost enough to convert me to the lap dog school of thought.'

'I'll bet.'

'Well, I'm keeping an open mind. The whole thing sounds so ludicrous, Mike. Like a Thurber fantasy. He was afraid to risk a quarrel with his wife by ducking her father's birthday party and the confrontation with Pauline Rourke, but he wasn't afraid to risk murder. Or is that simplifying too much?'

'It wasn't really much more complicated than that. Oh, he thought he had a grievance against Pauline Rourke, but it wouldn't have entered his head to kill her if he'd had the gumption to make the stand almost any other man in his position would have made. The attempt to kill Ivy Eastbrook was history repeating itself, more or less. The Thurber analogy is right on target. You know that cartoon of his called "House and Woman"? With the woman's face and hand looming up at the back of the house and the little man cringing up to the front steps? Well, imagine him walking up eagerly with a smile, and you have Geoffrey Cheyney alias Wallace Sayres.'

Cassandra laughed. 'I guess it isn't really funny, but what else is there to do except cry? If he's really as bad as that, I don't see why he ran out on Ivy Eastbrook. She must have done a good job of keeping him down on all fours. He should have been deliriously happy.'

'Ivy never lets go of the whip, and good mommies have to hand out rewards as well as punishment. Elizabeth would play the game better. She'd dole out lots of petting and caressing in return for that slavish devotion. *Noblesse oblige.*'

'What a crew!'

'What a crew.' The echo was bitter. 'What a case. What carnage. Think of it. Pauline Rourke dead. Jessie Weems a cinch to kick off any day now in a prison hospital instead of drinking herself to death quietly and harmlessly, as she would have done if she'd been let alone. Grace Weevil, getting a couple of rungs up on that tortuous climb to self-respect only to have the ladder yanked from under her, and what are the odds she'll ever set foot on it again? Ivy Eastbrook, who hates herself anyway, left with the knowledge that none of this would have happened if once upon a time a shark hadn't tried to mate with a minnow. And Cheyney himself, blasting a cosy little berth to hell for no damn reason.'

'I don't quite follow that. Fear of exposure provided a substantial motive, as motives go. Grand larceny and bigamy aren't petty crimes.'

'No, they aren't. Most people would have fallen all over themselves to bring them up to the light. But not Pauline Rourke, who had her own code of ethics. She wouldn't have given him away. She would have gone through that week-end making all the proper noises, holing up in the library with *Town and Country* and the *Atlantic Monthly*, and when it was all over she would have laughed herself silly about it. In private.'

'You're probably right. A joke at the irony of fate wouldn't have been less of a joke because she couldn't share it. Not for her. But you can't be sure, Mike. She might have been feeling bilious that week-end and leaped at the chance to score off Adrian Lefebvre.'

'No, I can't be sure. Except that she was scoring off

Adrian Lefebvre all along. And off Ivy Eastbrook. They were both dependent on her. It's a dangerous game, rubbing shoulders with unrestricted egotism. I wonder if she was aware that it was a game. Or that it was dangerous. No way of knowing. Life would be a hell of a lot simpler if we could see inside one another's heads.'

'It might be a little boring, though.' Cassandra got up, went out of the room, and returned in a moment with a glass of bourbon. She put the glass in Meredith's hand and curled up on the sofa again. 'Don't you think so?'

'I'm keeping an open mind.' He downed the drink in one swallow, kissed her cheek lightly, and, with a resigned sigh, crushed out his cigarette and picked up the sandwich. 'At any rate, your head is transparent.'

Cassandra laughed.